JON SABLE FREELANCE ™

CREATED, WRITTEN AND ILLUSTRATED BY

MIKE GRELL

PREFACE BY HOWARD CHAYKIN

FAWCETT COLUMBINE · NEW YORK

A Fawcett Columbine Book
Published by Ballantine Books
Copyright © 1983, 1987 by First Comics, Inc.
Preface Copyright © 1987 by Howard Chaykin
About the Author Copyright © 1987 by Mike Grell

All rights reserved under International and Pan-American Copyright
Conventions. Published in the United States by Ballantine Books,
a division of Random House, Inc., New York, and simultaneously
in Canada by Random House of Canada Limited, Toronto.

Published by Ballantine Books, a division of Random House, Inc.,
under exclusive license of First Comics, Inc., owner of
world-wide rights to the property *Jon Sable, Freelance.*

Jon Sable, Freelance and

FIRST
COMICS
®

are trademarks of First Comics, Inc.

Based on the original publications,
Jon Sable, Freelance, issues #1 through #6,
published by First Comics, Inc.

Library of Congress Catalog Card Number: 87-91165

ISBN: 0-449-90264-1

Cover design by Richard Aquan
Book design by Alex Jay/Studio J
Manufactured in the United States of America
First Edition: September 1987
10 9 8 7 6 5 4 3 2 1

TABLE OF CONTENTS

1

THE IRON MONSTER

2

DEATH IS A BUM DEAL

3

A STORM OVER EDEN

4

BATTLEMASK

5

KILLZONE

6

A DEADLY SHADE OF N VIOLET

CREDITS

JON SABLE, FREELANCE
Created, Written & Illustrated
by Mike Grell

THE IRON MONSTER
Janice Cohen, Colors
Peter Iro, Letters

DEATH IS A BUM DEAL
Janice Cohen, Colors
Peter Iro, Letters

A STORM OVER EDEN
Janice Cohen, Colors
Peter Iro, Letters

BATTLEMASK
Janice Cohen, Colors
Peter Iro, Letters

KILLZONE
Janice Cohen, Colors
Peter Iro, Letters

A DEADLY SHADE OF VIOLENT
Bruce Patterson, Colors
Peter Iro, Letters

All stories in this volume
edited by Mike Gold.

Based on the original publications,
Jon Sable, Freelance,
issues #1 through #6,
published by First Comics, Inc.

PREFACE

If you were ever to ask John Q. American to describe the average comic book creator—and actually stopped to think about it—you'd probably get something resembling a cross between Gepetto and Frankenstein (who, if you think about it, share a great deal—hmmm—but I digress...).

Fortunately or unfortunately—the reality doesn't live up to the fantasy. As a group we bear no likeness to kindly puppeteers, or monster makers. For the most part, we comics creators are pretty normal guys (and gals)—with an extra-normal means by which to act out our fantasy lives.

Most, if not all, of our heroic—not to say super-heroic—creations are simply extensions of our humdrum and occasionally chubby lives. Of course, some of us have different fantasies—mine, for example, don't include dressing up in tights and beating the snot out of evildoers—but, generally speaking, our two-dimensional heroes are "wish-dreams" of ourselves, embroidered with all those wonderful attributes we'd love others to see in us.

Which brings me to Mike Grell—and why he makes me mad as hell.

At first glance, you'd class Mike with the afore-mentioned crowd of craftsmen who, as Milton Caniff puts it, "ply the ink-stained trade." He looks like one of the guys. But while "the guys" were sending their creations to Hell and back to rescue the Universe, or whatever, Mike sent his boy, Sable, on safari in Africa—and then followed up the comic version with his own visit to the veldt—in person!

Understand—I'm not saying he's showing off. I'm sure Mike Grell would have started beating around the bush even if he hadn't created *Jon Sable, Freelance*. The fact remains that he *did* create Sable—Hunter of Men, At Home In Any Jungle, Urban or Primordial—and that Mike *did* go off to Africa to test his mettle against his creation's standards.

And those standards are pretty high, indeed. The *Jon Sable, Freelance* package—Sable himself, B. B. Flemm, Eden Kendall, et al.—is far and away the most complex and fully realized of Grell's creations. Jon himself is clearly a comic book version of Mike's fantasy self—but a fantasy self with a resonance of a heart and a human scale not found in too many of today's American comics.

The human scale is the key to *JSF*. We've all had our fill of grimly-vengeful-macho-killer-ninnies in comics, movies, and television—characters that lay waste to three-fourths of the civilized world with the same kind of emotional involvement most of us bring to opting for chocolate over strawberry. Sorry—that just isn't the territory explored in this book. In *Sable*, Grell has given us a genuine anomaly in the context of pulp paper heroes: Jon is a living, breathing mass of contradictions—not just one more masked avenger with the sort of problems we'd all give our eyeteeth for—and the majority of those contradictions come straight from the heart of his creator.

Now, I don't know squat about Mike's political views—and I could care less. What I do know is that Mike is the butchest, machoest guy I know personally—you know, guns, hunting, wildlife painting, the whole deal. The real secret is that he's also the mushiest he-man you could hope to meet, because under the paunch held tight by his Red Army buckle (ask him about that sometime...) beats the bleeding heart of a real soft touch—who just happens to own an elephant gun (don't ask him about that...).

So—why am I mad as hell, you ask? Well...

Before Sable, Mike was best known for superhero and sword & sorcery strips, and I was best known for bitching and moaning about the utter dearth of straight adventure features—with the obvious intention of returning that genre to its rightful popularity with my own *American Flagg*. Then, all of a sudden, out of the blue, comes ol' Mike Grell with *his* adventure strip, beating me to the punch—as well as laying down a bit of groundwork for Flagg to stand on. So—he not only gets his book out first, but I owe him for warming up the audience.

Have a heart, Mike—huh?

Howard Chaykin
June 1987

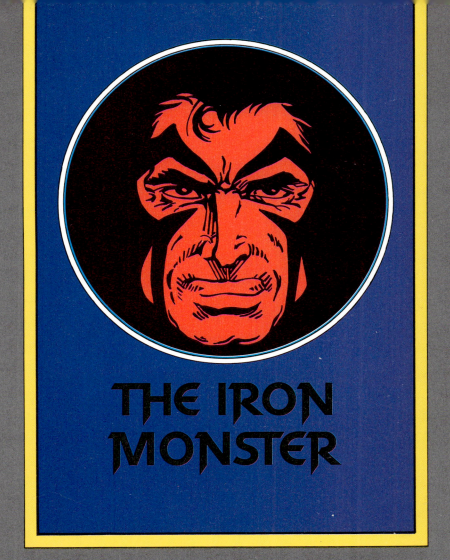

THE IRON
MONSTER

CREATED, WRITTEN
AND ILLUSTRATED BY
MIKE GRELL

EDITED BY
MIKE GOLD

COLORS BY
JANICE COHEN

LETTERS BY
PETER IRO

...BUT WHAT GAVE YOU THE IDEA FOR STORIES ABOUT *LEPRECHAUNS* LIVING IN *CENTRAL PARK?*

I THOUGHT IT WOULD BE FUN TO SEE WHAT HAPPENS TO THE "SMALLEST" MINORITY GROUP IN THE WORLD.

FOR INSTANCE, THEY HAD TO *"LOWER"* THEIR STANDARDS FOR EMPLOYMENT--

--THE ONLY QUALIFICATION IS THAT YOU MUST BE *VERY SHORT!*

STAND BY, ONE.

HA! HA! HA! THAT'S WHERE YOU GET GUYS LIKE *JOSE* AND *KAREEM,* AND MY FAVORITE...*BENNY COHEN.*

THEY PRONOUNCE IT *COHAN!*

ALL OF WHICH ADDS UP TO TEN DIGIT SALES FIGURES IN THE CHILDREN'S BOOK MARKET FOR *B.B. FLEMM.*

ONE LAST QUESTION, JUST FOR THE RECORD...

...WHAT DOES THE "B.B." STAND FOR?

BUFORD BERTRAND.

TAKE ONE.

WHILE THE PRESIDENT AND THE FIRST LADY CONTINUE THEIR VACATION IN CALIFORNIA, PREPARATIONS ARE BEING MADE FOR TOMORROW EVENING'S CEREMONIES OUTSIDE THE U.N.

EXIT

AS WITH ANY PRESIDENTIAL VISIT, THE QUESTION OF SECURITY IS FOREMOST IN THE MINDS OF THE NEW YORK POLICE.

JESSICA PHILLIPS SPOKE WITH POLICE OFFICIALS EARLIER TODAY.

1.

ACTIVATE
HOGAN'S
ALLEY

RANDOM
PROGRAM
LEVEL 12

DO YOU
FEEL
LUCKY,
PUNK?

VERY
FUNNY.

DRAW!

4.

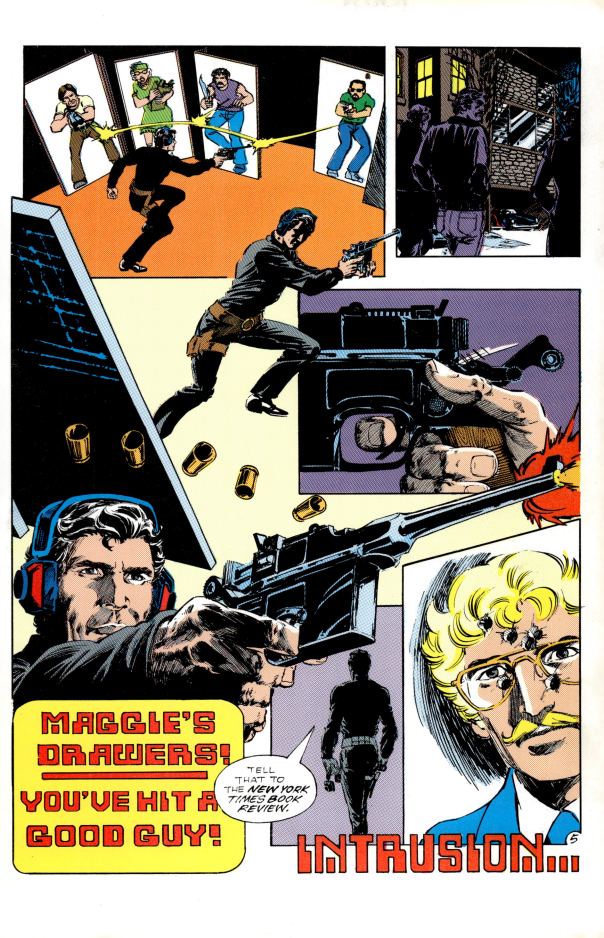

INTRUSION...INTRUSION

LETTERER:
PETER IRO
COLORIST:
JANICE COHEN

THE IRON

...INTRUSION...INTRUSI

JON Sable FREELANCE

created, written & illustrated by: MIKE GRELL

MONSTER!

EDITOR: MIKE GOLD

TALK TO ME.

WHERE ARE MY MEN?

IN A DUMPSTER OUT IN THE ALLEY... UNLESS THE GARBAGE TRUCK WAS LATE TONIGHT.

WELL, YOU'RE BETTER THAN I WAS TOLD...THEY WERE *SUPPOSED* TO BE MY BEST.

THEN YOU'RE IN A LOT OF TROUBLE.

TAKE A WALK, SAM.

DO YOU KNOW ME?

I KNOW WHO YOU *LOOK* LIKE.

GOT ANY *ID*?

WILL *THIS* DO?

AMERICAN EXPRESS

YOU'RE SUPPOSED TO BE IN CALIFORNIA...

I WAS *SUPPOSED* TO WIN AN *OSCAR*, TOO...

BUT THAT DOESN'T MAKE IT *SO*!

WHAT DO YOU WANT WITH ME?

OUR INFORMATION INDICATES AN *ASSASINATION ATTEMPT* WILL BE MADE DURING TOMORROW NIGHT'S CEREMONY AT THE UNITED NATIONS.

CANCEL.

OUT OF THE QUESTION. NOT AFTER THE *LIBYAN HIT SQUAD* FIASCO!

WHAT MAKES YOU THINK I'LL TAKE THE JOB?

I DIDN'T EVEN *VOTE* FOR YOU.

YOU DIDN'T VOTE *AT ALL!* I'VE SEEN YOUR FILE, MR. SABLE--OR SHOULD I SAY, *MR. FLEMM?*

THE LIBRARY OF CONGRESS HAS YOUR PEN NAME ON RECORD. IT ALL GOES INTO THE *CENTRAL COMPUTER.*

I WONDER WHAT WOULD HAPPEN TO A 3.5 MILLION DOLLAR-A-YEAR CHILDREN'S BOOK BUSINESS IF THE KIDDIES FOUND OUT--

--NOT TO MENTION WHAT YOUR...*LESS INNOCENT*...ASSOCIATES WOULD DO IF THEY DIS- COVERED THE CHINK IN YOUR ARMOR.

HOW--?

THAT'S *LITTERING.*

THAT'S *BLACKMAIL.*

I'M PREPARED TO PAY YOU.

IT'S *STILL* BLACKMAIL.

I HAVE AN INCURABLE SENSE OF DRAMA.

WHY NOT LET YOUR PEOPLE HANDLE IT?

YOU SAW WHAT "MY PEOPLE" ARE LIKE. I WANT THE *BEST.*

BESIDES, YOU MAY HAVE A *PERSONAL INTEREST* IN THIS CASE.

WE'VE IDENTIFIED THE HIT MAN AS *MILO JACKSON!*

10.

ARE YOU SURE IT'S *HIM*?

POSITIVE. WE TRACED HIM TO A RENTED OFFICE NEAR THE U.N.

WE STAKED IT OUT, BUT HE HASN'T BEEN BACK.

O.K., I'LL TAKE THE JOB.

BUT IT'S GOING TO *COST*!

IT USUALLY DOES, MR. SABLE.

HALF NOW... HALF WHEN THE JOB IS DONE.

HOW MUCH?

NOT CASH.

THERE'S A CERTAIN *POLICE CAPTAIN* WHO'D LIKE TO SEE MY *HIDE* NAILED TO HIS WALL...

AND IF I CROSS HIM AGAIN, HE'LL *HAVE* IT!

FIRST I WANT A *CARTE BLANCHE* LICENSE TO OPERATE.

DONE! WHAT ELSE?

WE'LL SETTLE THAT WHEN THE JOB'S DONE.

YOU SEE... I ALSO HAVE AN INCURABLE SENSE OF DRAMA.

GIVE MY REGARDS TO BONZO.

BONZO IS *DEAD*, MR. SABLE.

11.

A NAME FROM THE PAST...

A SOUVENIR OF BYGONE GLORY.

1972 OLYMPI... MU...

MILO JACKSON

SILVER MEDAL

A MEMORY OF BITTER HATRED.

RHODESIA...1979...

HEY, JONNY-BOY-- HOW'S THE WING?

STILL A LITTLE STIFF, MILO.

TOO BAD, CAP'N.

I WISH I WERE GOING ALONG.

SO DO I, JONNY, YOU'VE NO IDEA

DON'T WORRY. WE'LL GIVE 'EM HELL FOR YOU.

VIVE LA MORTE! VIVE LA GUERRE! VIVA LA SACRE MERCENAIRE!

THEY WERE MORE THAN FRIENDS, THEY WERE COMRADES-AT-ARMS... MEN WHO SHARED DEATH AS THEY SHARED LIFE, AND RAISED THEIR VOICES IN THE AGE-OLD TOAST...

12.

WHAT SOME MEN DO FOR A *CAUSE*, OTHERS DO FOR *MONEY*. BUT THERE IS YET ANOTHER KIND OF MAN, WHO LIVES ONLY FOR THE JOY OF DANGER. THIS WAS MILO JACKSON.

ANT-TERRORIST PATROLS ARE THE DEADLIEST HUNT FOR THE MOST DANGEROUS GAME, AND MILO JACKSON WAS MOST OFTEN FOUND IN HIS FAVORITE POSITION... *THE POINT!*

THE POINT WAS WHAT HE DID BEST... THAT'S WHY THE *AMBUSH* WAS SO UNEXPECTED.

NOT A SHOT WAS FIRED IN DEFENSE.

ABOVE ALL, MILO JACKSON KNEW HOW TO TAKE CARE OF MILO JACKSON.

FIVE MONTHS LATER THE *TRUTH* WAS LEARNED FROM A CAPTURED TERRORIST.

UNTIL NOW.

RINGGG!

BY THEN, MILO HAD DISAPPEARED.

13.

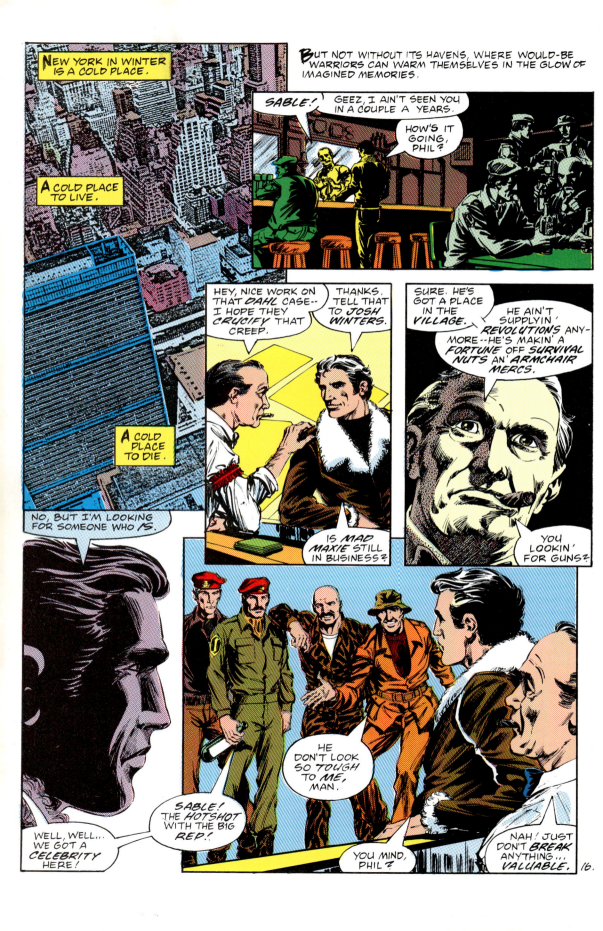

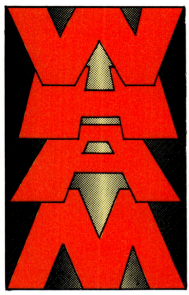

THANKS FOR THE TIP, PHIL...

SEE YA.

THREE A.M.

SIXTEEN HOURS UNTIL THE CEREMONY AT THE U.N.

SURVIVAL SPECIALTIES

NO TIME TO WASTE.

PLENTY OF TIME TO KILL!

17.

18.

FOUR A.M.

SURVIVAL SPECIALTIES

POLICE
2071

YOU GOT A LOTTA *GUTS*, SABLE.

YOU'VE GOT A LOT OF *TROUBLE* ON YOUR HANDS, CAPTAIN. THAT'S WHY I *CALLED* YOU.

FREEZ DRIED CHICKE

15% OFF

AMO

YOU'RE *HEAD OF SECURITY* FOR THE PRESIDENT'S SPEECH AT THE U.N. YOU'RE GOING TO HAVE TO *CANCEL* IT.

CANCEL IT? WHY THE HELL *SHOULD* I?

BECAUSE *HE WON'T...*

7·mm / 300WBY
168 gr. Speer
72 gr. IMR-4350

...AND A GUY NAMED *MILO JACKSON* IS GOING TO DO *THIS* TO HIS *HEAD!*

WHAT'S *YOUR* CONNECTION?

CALL ME A *CONCERNED CITIZEN.*

19

"CONCERNED CITIZENS" DON'T GET INVOLVED IN HOMICIDE.

ASSUME THE POSITION, PUNK!

WHAT'S THIS GOING TO PROVE?

MAYBE YOU ICED MAXIE... TRIED TO PIN IT ON THIS MILO JACKSON

WELL, WELL, LOOK WHAT I FOUND. EVER HEARD OF THE SULLIVAN LAW?

I'VE GOT A LICENSE.

NOT ANYMORE, PUNK.

COME ON WINTERS! YOU KNOW VERY WELL MAXIE WAS STABBED, NOT SHOT!

NOT UNTIL THE CORONER SAYS SO.

MEANWHILE, YOU SIT IT OUT IN THE SLAMMER AND I GET A LITTLE PEACE AND QUIET.

WANNA BET?

DO YOURSELF A FAVOR AND CALL THE NUMBER ON THIS CARD.

20.

WE GOT THE **PRESIDENT** AND EVERY **BIGWIG** YOU CAN IMAGINE COMING HERE IN **TWO HOURS**, AND **LOOK** AT THIS **MESS!**

ORANGE PAINT ALL OVER **EVERYTHING!**

AND UP THERE IT EVEN LOOKS LIKE THEY TOOK A **BALL PEEN** HAMMER TO IT!

WHEN DID IT HAPPEN?

LAST NIGHT... EARLY THIS MORNING... I DON'T KNOW.

T.V. CAMERAS COMIN'--!

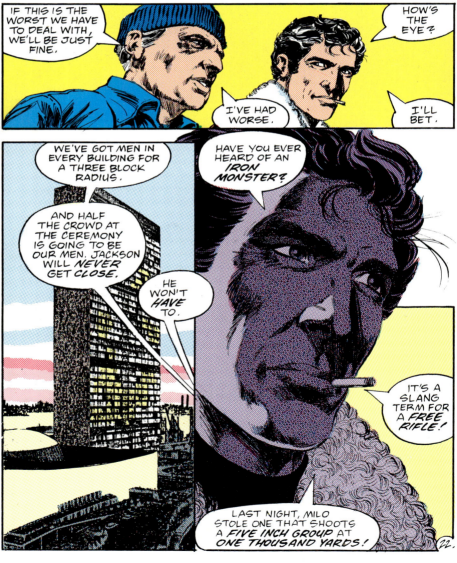

IF THIS IS THE WORST WE HAVE TO DEAL WITH, WE'LL BE JUST FINE.

HOW'S THE EYE?

I'VE HAD WORSE.

I'LL BET.

WE'VE GOT MEN IN EVERY BUILDING FOR A THREE BLOCK RADIUS.

HAVE YOU EVER HEARD OF AN **IRON MONSTER?**

AND HALF THE CROWD AT THE CEREMONY IS GOING TO BE OUR MEN. JACKSON WILL **NEVER** GET **CLOSE.**

HE WON'T **HAVE** TO.

IT'S A SLANG TERM FOR A **FREE RIFLE!**

LAST NIGHT, MILO STOLE ONE THAT SHOOTS A **FIVE INCH GROUP** AT **ONE THOUSAND YARDS!**

22.

THE MARKS ON THE WALL ARE *BULLET HOLES.*

Oh, lordy.

DARKNESS SHROUDS THE SENTINEL OF WORLD PEACE, BUT PREPARATIONS FOR THE EVENING'S ACTIVITIES CONTINUE UNCHECKED BY THE THREAT OF DEATH.

FIVE P.M.

WHICH ROOM?

832. ON THE CORNER.

IT'S *COLD* IN HERE.

WERE THOSE WINDOWS OPEN WHEN YOU FOUND IT?

WE HAVEN'T TOUCHED A THING. DIDN'T WANT TO SCARE HIM AWAY.

NICE VIEW OF THE U.N.

BUT YOU CAN'T EVEN *SEE* THE CEREMONY SITE FROM HERE.

WANT SOME *COFFEE?* I'VE BEEN COLD ALL DAY.

NO THANKS. I'LL WAIT.

DAMMIT, MILO-- WHY AREN'T YOU HERE?

IT'S A *PERFECT* SETUP-- T.V. LIGHTS...LOTS OF NICE FLAGS TO HELP JUDGE THE *WIND DRIFT* OF YOUR BULLET.

BUT YOU *CAN'T SEE* THAT DAMN *WALL* FROM HERE!

23

SO WHERE THE HELL WERE YOU *SHOOTING FROM* LAST N--!

AW, MAN!

FIVE-FORTY-FIVE P.M.

GREAT! NO BACK-UP!

I HOPE THAT AGENT *ENJOYS* HIS COFFEE!

THREE BLOCKS, A LONG WAY TO RUN IN THE BITTER COLD, WITH YOUR LUNGS CURSING EVERY CIGARETTE YOU HAD EVER SMOKED.

...AND *I'M* NOT STUPID ENOUGH TO FALL FOR HIS *TRAP!*

HE LEFT THE *ELEVATOR* DOWN!

HE'S NOT *STUPID* ENOUGH TO *FORGET...*

FIVE-FIFTY FIVE P.M.

24.

25.

26.

27.

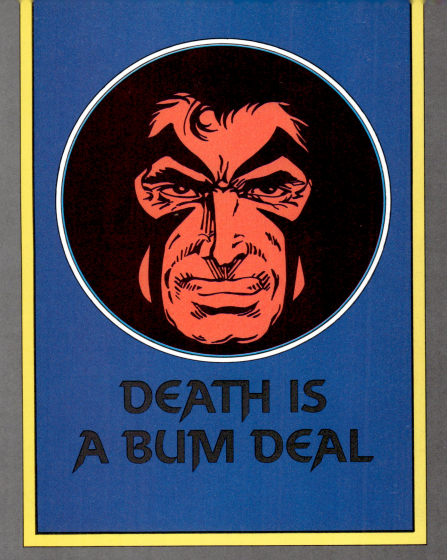

DEATH IS
A BUM DEAL

CREATED, WRITTEN
AND ILLUSTRATED BY
MIKE GRELL

EDITED BY
MIKE GOLD

COLORS BY
JANICE COHEN

LETTERS BY
PETER IRO

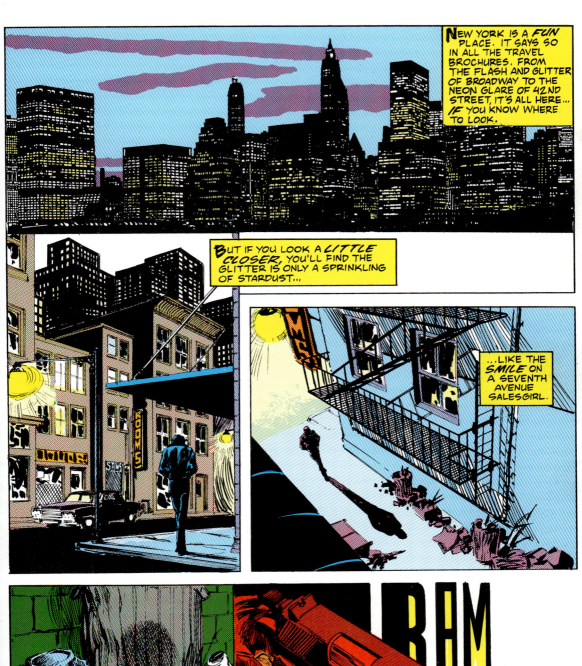

NEW YORK IS A *FUN* PLACE. IT SAYS SO IN ALL THE TRAVEL BROCHURES. FROM THE FLASH AND GLITTER OF BROADWAY TO THE NEON GLARE OF 42ND STREET, IT'S ALL HERE... *IF* YOU KNOW WHERE TO LOOK.

BUT IF YOU LOOK A *LITTLE CLOSER*, YOU'LL FIND THE GLITTER IS ONLY A SPRINKLING OF STARDUST...

...LIKE THE *SMILE* ON A SEVENTH AVENUE SALESGIRL.

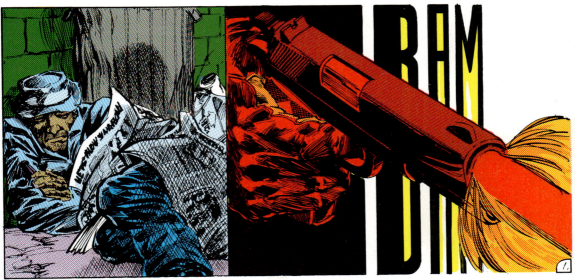

BAM

BOWERY SLAYER STRIKES AGAIN!

FIFTH VICTIM IDENTIFIED.

HAVE A NICE DAY.

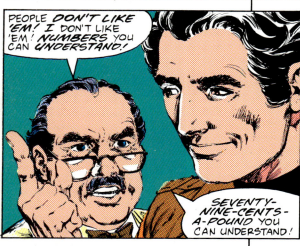

PEOPLE *DON'T LIKE 'EM!* I DON'T LIKE 'EM! *NUMBERS* YOU CAN *UNDERSTAND!*

SEVENTY-NINE-CENTS-A-POUND YOU CAN UNDERSTAND!

OKAY, GRANDMA --THE *CASH!*

C'MON! C'MON! WE AIN'T GOT ALL NIGHT.

SO WHO KNOWS FROM LITTLE *LINES* YOU GOTTA WAVE OVER A *THING?*

DEATH IS A

LETTERER: *PETE IRO*

COLORIST:

RAISING THE PRICES AGAIN, MR. GOLDBLUM?

LIKE ALWAYS, MR. SABLE.

THEY CHANGE SO FAST EVEN *I* CAN'T KEEP UP.

A HUNDRED TIMES I TOLD HIM WE SHOULD GET A SCANNER.

SURE, LIKE YOUR BROTHER, THE *TYCOON*.

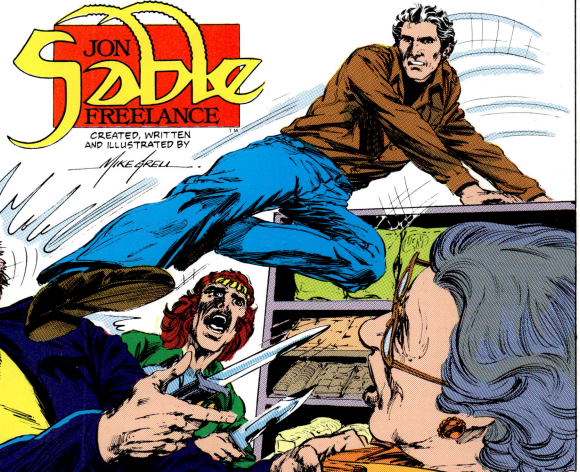

JON SABLE FREELANCE

CREATED, WRITTEN AND ILLUSTRATED BY

MIKE GRELL

BUM DEAL!

JANICE COHEN

EDITOR: *MIKE GOLD*

NEXT MORNING...

MR. FLEMM IS HERE TO SEE YOU, MS. KENDALL.

SEND HIM IN, STAN.

ABOUT TIME, HE'S AN HOUR LATE.

NOT SURPRISING. HE PUT IN A... *LONG, HARD NIGHT*

BOUNTYHUNTER FOILS HOLDUP

LET'S MAKE THIS *BRIEF*, SHALL WE?

AND GOOD MORNING TO YOU, MR. FLEMM.

B.B. FLEMM, I'D LIKE YOU TO MEET MYKE BLACKMON.

AH, YES, THE *ARTIST* CHAP.

HOW DO YOU DO, MR--!

MY GOD! YOU'RE A GIRL!

UH-HUH ALL OVER.

6.

I DIDN'T MEAN--!

THAT'S OKAY, I GET IT ALL THE TIME...ALONG WITH "HOW'S THE WEATHER UP THERE?"

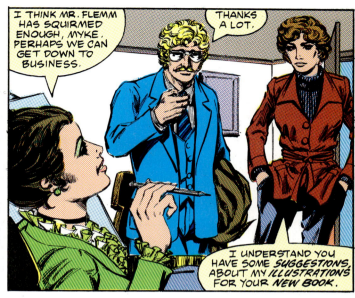

I THINK MR. FLEMM HAS SQUIRMED ENOUGH, MYKE. PERHAPS WE CAN GET DOWN TO BUSINESS.

THANKS A LOT.

I UNDERSTAND YOU HAVE SOME *SUGGESTIONS* ABOUT MY *ILLUSTRATIONS* FOR YOUR *NEW BOOK*.

I BROUGHT MY PRELIMINARY SKETCHES--

FUNNY, I NEVER KNEW YOU WERE A--

I'VE WORKED ON YOUR BOOKS FOR OVER *TWO YEARS*, MR. FLEMM--YOU NEVER *ASKED!*

UM...YES, WELL, I'M AFRAID I HAVE A RATHER BUSY SCHEDULE...

I'VE MADE A *LIST* OF CHANGES.

I'LL TAKE THAT.

I REALLY MUST BE OFF. NICE MEETING YOU, MS. BLACKMON!

THAT'S *MISS!*

DOES HE ALWAYS COME AND GO SO *FAST?*

NOT *ALWAYS!* 7.

WELL, I DIDN'T TAKE HALF A DAY OFF WORK FOR *NOTHING.*

I WOULDN'T FOLLOW HIM, MYKE--!

WELL, *I* WOULD!

BUT AS THE ANGRY ARTIST REACHES THE STREET...

DAMN! MISSED HIM!

TAXI!

FOLLOW THAT CAR!

YOU'RE *KIDDIN'* RIGHT!

DRIVE!

YOU'RE *NOT* KIDDIN'!

THE TRAIL OF THE ELUSIVE B.B. FLEMM LEADS TO A MODERN TOWNHOUSE NESTLED IN A QUIET BROWNSTONE NEIGHBORHOOD...

HOW MUCH?

FORGET IT, KID. TWENTY-SIX YEARS I BEEN DRIVIN' THIS HACK, AND THIS IS THE FIRST TIME ANYBODY TOLD ME "FOLLOW THAT CAR."

YES? UH-OH.

INFORM MR. FLEMM THAT *MISS BLACKMON* WOULD LIKE TO SPEAK TO HIM.

FLEMM? I'M AFRAID THERE'S BEEN SOME MISTAKE!

8.

A LITTLE OF **BOTH,** I GUESS.

FLEMM GETS OUT OF HAND SOMETIMES ...BUT HE SERVES A **PURPOSE.**

YOU SPEAK OF HIM AS IF HE WERE **SOMEONE ELSE.**

HE **IS.**

NOTHING **SCHIZO,** MIND YOU...

IT'S JUST THAT **MER-CENARIES** DON'T WRITE **CHILDREN'S BOOKS.**

LOOK, MR ...**WHATEVER**... I DON'T KNOW WHAT'S GOING ON HERE, AND I'M NOT SURE I **CARE!**

WHAT I **DO** CARE ABOUT IS MY **WORK,** AND I'VE ALREADY LOST HALF A DAY AT THE DRAWING BOARD BECAUSE OF YOU!

I'VE BEEN ILLUSTRATING YOUR BOOKS FOR **TWO YEARS** AND IN ALL THAT TIME YOU NEVER HAD **ONE WORD OF PRAISE!**

NOW THERE'S A **PROBLEM...NOW** I GET A **ROYAL AUDIENCE!**

I'M A **DAMN GOOD ARTIST,** MR. SABLE, AND IF YOU'D AT LEAST **WORK** WITH ME, THERE WOULDN'T **BE** ANY PROBLEMS...

YOU'RE RIGHT.

...BUT I NEED MORE THAN **TWO MINUTES** OF YOUR TI....!

HUH?

I SAID "YOU'RE RIGHT" -- THERE'S NO EXCUSE FOR BAD MANNERS. I APOLOGIZE.

11.

SIX YEARS AGO HE WAS A TOP RESEARCH ENGINEER FOR AN ELECTRONICS FIRM-- TWO DAYS AGO HE DIED A SKID ROW BUM.

SOME *NUT* BLEW HIS BRAINS OUT. BUT HE *CRAWLED* INTO THAT BOTTLE ON HIS OWN.

THEN THERE'S NO REASON TO BELIEVE HIS DEATH WAS ANYTHING BUT ANOTHER RANDOM KILLING.

THAT'S WHAT THE *POLICE* SAID.

SO WHAT'S ONE *BUM* MORE OR LESS, RIGHT?

THAT OLD BUM USED TO BOUNCE ME ON HIS KNEE AND TELL ME BEDTIME STORIES.

SO WHO CARES, RIGHT?

I SAW HIM MEND A BIRD'S BROKEN WING...AND WATCHED HIM CRY THE DAY IT FLEW AWAY.

THAT OLD *DRUNK* WAS MY *FATHER*, DAMN IT.

I *WANT* THE *ANIMAL* WHO *KILLED* HIM!

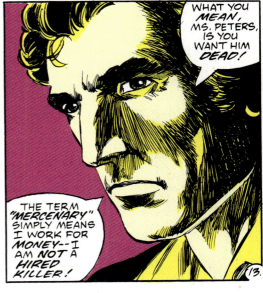

WHAT YOU *MEAN*, MS. PETERS, IS YOU WANT HIM *DEAD!*

THE TERM *"MERCENARY"* SIMPLY MEANS I WORK FOR *MONEY*-- I AM *NOT* A *HIRED KILLER!*

13.

WHERE WILL YOU START?

THE *POLICE* DON'T EVEN--!

DON'T SELL THEM *SHORT*, MS. PETERS.

ODDS ARE THEY HAVE PLENTY OF CLUES...THEY JUST WON'T TALK ABOUT THEM.

THE FIRST THING I HAVE TO DO IS TO FIND SOMEONE WHO *WILL.*

I'LL BE IN TOUCH.

MEANWHILE, I'VE WRITTEN A NUMBER HERE THAT YOU CAN CALL WHEN YOU NEED HELP.

WHAT IS IT?

ALCOHOLICS ANONYMOUS.

Shortly...

I'M A FILE CLERK, SABLE... WHAT DO I KNOW ABOUT SOME NUT WASTING BUMS ON SKID ROW?

YOU'RE A LOUSY LIAR, HAROLD.

...BUT YOU'D HAVE BEEN A HELL OF A COP...

...IF YOU'D BEEN *SIX-FOOT-THREE* INSTEAD OF *THREE-FOOT SIX!*

OKAY, GET THIS...

IT *AIN'T* A NUT! IT AIN'T EVEN *ONE GUY!*

A *GANG?*

THAT'S WHAT THE *D.A.* THINKS. TAKE A LOOK.

15.

THERE'S NO SUCH THING AS A SUNSET ON THE BOWERY...

...SOMETIME DURING THE AFTERNOON THE SUN DUCKS BEHIND A BUILDING, AND THAT'S IT.

AT LEAST YOU CAN'T SEE THE DIRT AS CLEARLY IN THE DARK.

...UNLESS YOU'RE AN UNDERCOVER COP NAMED PHIL WALKER, LOOKING FOR A KILLER.

THEN, YOU LIVE IN IT.

AND SOMETIMES, YOU DIE IN IT...

17.

HOURS LATER...

THAT'LL BE ALL FOR NOW, SABLE-- BUT STICK AROUND IN CASE WE NEED YOU.

SORRY ABOUT YOUR MAN, CAPTAIN.

JUST DO US A FAVOR AND STAY OUT OF THE ALLEYS, SABLE, *YOU* ATTRACT *TROUBLE* LIKE A *MAGNET!*

YEAH.

BALLISTICS

FINISHED WITH THE BALLISTICS REPORT ON THE SLUG THEY TOOK OUT OF WALKER?

JUST ABOUT. SEE FOR YOURSELF.

JUST LIKE ALL THE REST... .45 ACP.

AND JUST LIKE ALL THE REST, NOTHING MATCHES--IT'S A DIFFERENT GUN AGAIN.

GOD, DO YOU SMELL BAD!

DON'T YOU *UNDERCOVER* GUYS EVER *BATHE--?*

HEY! YOU'RE NOT A *COP!*

NEVER SAID I *WAS.*

GET THE HELL OUT OF HERE BEFORE I HAVE YOU *BUSTED!*

IS THAT ANYWAY TO TALK TO SOMEONE WHO BROUGHT YOU A *PRESENT?*

TELL *JOSH WINTERS* SANTA WAS A LITTLE LATE.

HO HO HO.

18.

THE POLICE ARE ON THE *WRONG TRACK*, MS. PETERS...

WHAT DO YOU MEAN?

NO TWO SLUGS MATCHED, SO THEY'RE LOOKING FOR A GANG OF .45-TOTING KILLERS.

I'M CONVINCED IT REALLY *IS* JUST *ONE MAN!*

BUT HOW--?

ANY G.I. CAN *CHANGE BARRELS* ON A .45 IN LESS THAN *SIXTY SECONDS.*

BUT THE *REST* OF THE GUN STAYS THE *SAME.*

THE KILLER IS USING ONE WITH A FIRING PIN THAT STRIKES THE PRIMER A LITTLE OFF-CENTER.

THE KILLER WAS CAREFUL TO *PICK UP* ALL HIS *EMPTY BRASS...*

...BUT THE CASE *I* PICKED UP IN THE ALLEY LAST NIGHT *MATCHES* THE ONE FOUND AT THE SCENE OF YOUR FATHER'S DEATH.

SAME *GUN*... SAME *KILLER!* NO QUESTION.

THAT STILL DOESN'T TELL ME *WHO* THE KILLER IS, OR *WHY.*

MAYBE I'LL FIND OUT TONIGHT BUT FIRST, I NEED SOME SLEEP.

MAY I MAKE A SUGGESTION?

YOU COULD USE A *BATH*, TOO!

YOU SMELL *AWFUL!*

19

THE DEADLIEST OF PREDATORS WALKS BY NIGHT...

CLOAKED IN VELVET DARKNESS, HE STALKS THE CONCRETE CANYONS ...SENSES STRAINING...

...KNOWING THAT THE QUARRY IS THERE...

...SOMEWHERE...

...WAITING!

20.

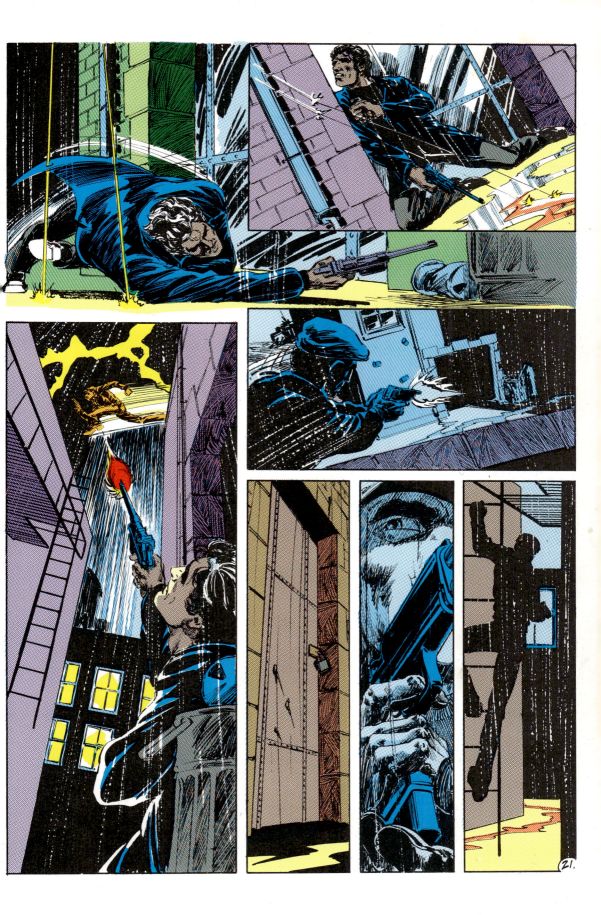

21.

22.

THAT'S THE BEST I CAN DO, SABLE.

YOU NEED A DOCTOR.

NOT UNTIL I FINISH THIS!

I'VE GOT THE WHO AND THE HOW BUT I STILL DON'T KNOW WHY.

THAT SHOULDER IS GOING TO LAY YOU UP FOR A WHILE.

NOT BEFORE I FIND OUT WHAT'S BEHIND THIS...

...AND WHY I WAS SET UP!

SET UP?!

SAME GUN... DIFFERENT M.O. --HE SHOT FROM A ROOF-TOP INSTEAD OF CLOSE UP.

HE WAS AFTER ME THIS TIME!

QUESTION IS HOW HE KNEW I WAS--!

LOOK AT THIS!

THAT'S A NEW BARREL, BUT LOOK AT THESE MARKS NEAR THE MUZZLE!

LOOKS LIKE THEY WERE CUT IN.

MAYBE THE GUY WAS TRYING TO SCREW UP THE BALLISTICS BY ADDING LITTLE LINES.

WHY BOTHER? IF HE CHANGED BARRELS FOR EVERY HIT?

WHAT DOES HE GAIN BY ADDING THOSE LINES? WHY--?

OH, MAN!

IT'S ALMOST TOO WILD TO BELIEVE.

THIS IS JON SABLE--I NEED A FAVOR.

23.

TRY THIS.

CAN YOU BREAK IT, HAROLD?

WITH MR. FRIEDMAN'S COMPUTER... IT'S A SNAP!

IT WORKS!

13599769

I'VE SEEN THIS BEFORE... IT'S A SIMPLE NUMERICAL CODE LIKE THEY USED IN WW TWO--

--EACH NUMBER STANDS FOR A LETTER.

MINUTES LATER...

KUR

HERE IT COMES! HERE IT COMES!

KURT RUNGLUS   PETER WILSON
RT 2 BOX 205   KENT, CT
OTTO JURGENS   EDWARD PHIPPS
10268 PALM BLVD. MIAMI, FL
HEINRICH FASS   JAIMES CLARK
1321 OAK ST.   PITTSBURGH, PA
KARL SCHTAFFLE CALVIN MITCHELL
802 S. HIL

MY GOD!

I KNOW THOSE MEN!

25.

DON'T BOTHER TO PACK.

YOU WON'T NEED IT WHERE YOU'RE GOING.

GUTEN MORGEN, OBERLEUTNANT SCHTAFFLE.

THEY FOUND MY... "ASSOCIATE'S" BODY ON SKID ROW.

YOU'RE MORE... *RESILIENT* THAN I IMAGINED.

BUT *NOT INVULNERABLE,* I SEE. THAT'S REFRESHING!

WELL, WHEN JOSH WINTERS GETS HERE, DON'T LET ON, OKAY?

YOU'LL SPOIL MY *IMAGE.*

YOU'RE NOT GOING TO *SHOOT* ME?

THAT DEPENDS ON HOW *ENTERTAINING* YOU CAN BE.

26.

WHAT TIPPED YOU OFF?

WHY DIDN'T THE COURIER JUST *HAND* YOU THE CODES?

PART OF OUR SECURITY, WE *NEVER* MET-- I MERELY INTERCEPTED THE INFORMATION.

BUT *YOU* SET ME UP.

I PASSED WORD THROUGH OUR NETWORK...WE ARE A *LARGE* GROUP.

PASSING CODED INFORMATION ON BULLETS IS TRICKY-- YOU HAVE TO BE SURE THE *RIGHT MAN* RECEIVES IT.

WHO ELSE BUT THE *POLICE BALLISTICS EXPERT* WOULD GET HIS HANDS ON *ALL* THE SLUGS?

I KNOW... I'VE SEEN YOUR *MEMBERSHIP ROSTER.*

YOUR NAME WAS THERE, TOO, ONE OF YOUR FORMER *"GUESTS"* RECOGNIZED IT.

CALVIN MITCHELL...ALIAS *OBER-LEUTNANT KARL SCHTAEFLE, SS!* YOU SLAUGHTERED A LOT OF PEOPLE AT *AUSCHWITZ!*

THOUSANDS... BUT THEN I WAS TRANSFERRED TO *RUSSIA* AFTER ONLY *FIVE* MONTHS!

AFTER THE WAR YOUR CIA WAS WILLING TO...FORGET.

IN EXCHANGE FOR *ANTI-SOVIET* ACTIVITIES, MANY OF US WERE *GIVEN* ENTRY TO THE U.S....ALONG WITH *NEW* IDENTITIES.

SO YOU WENT UNDERCOVER...A *SLEEPER*... WAITING ALMOST *FORTY* YEARS FOR THE *REICH* TO RISE AGAIN.

WAITING FOR THE *SIGNAL* FROM YOUR *LEADER.*

WHO IS IT? MENGELE? BORMANN? HITLER?

IT DOESN'T MATTER, IT'S GOING TO *HAPPEN.*

THE STRIFE IN THE MIDEAST...ECONOMIC CHAOS IN THE WEST-- THE TIME IS *RIPE* FOR A *NEW ORDER!* 27.

OUR CODE SYSTEM WAS DE-VELOPED BY AN ENGINEER NAMED *RAYMOND PETERS.*

YOU'RE BEING *VERY* COOPERA-TIVE, SCHTAFFLE...BUT I *KNOW* WHAT YOU'RE *THINKING.*

HE THOUGHT HE WAS WORKING FOR THE *ARMY,* YOU SEE--BUT HE STILL HAD TO BE *ELIMINATED.*

I'M *BLEEDING* AGAIN....

...MAYBE GETTING A LITTLE *SHOCKY!*

THAT WAS EASY. WHO EVEN *NOTICES* THE DEATH OF A *BUM*...ESPECIALLY IF HE'S *FIFTH* IN A LONG LINE OF "RANDOM" KILLINGS?

MAYBE I'LL *PASS OUT* BEFORE WINTERS GETS HERE...

...AND THEN MAYBE YOU'LL *BLOW MY BRAINS OUT.*

BLAM

MAYBE YOU'RE RIGHT.

MR. SABLE...YOUR OVERSEAS CALL TO *SIMON WIESENTHAL* IS READY.

MR. SABLE--?

NEXT ISSUE--
AT LAST!
The ORIGIN!

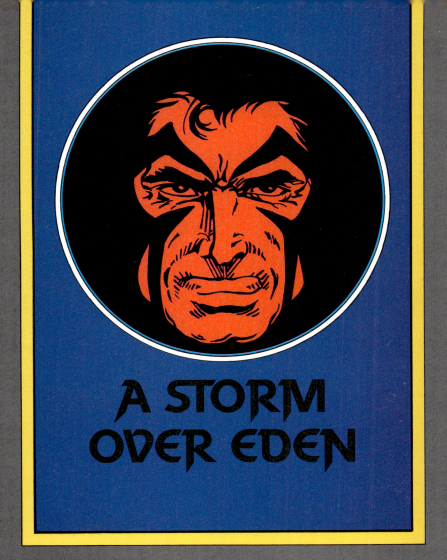

A STORM OVER EDEN

CREATED, WRITTEN
AND ILLUSTRATED BY
MIKE GRELL

EDITED BY
MIKE GOLD

COLORS BY
JANICE COHEN

LETTERS BY
PETER IRO

WHERE IS HE?

OUT OF TOWN.

SWELL! I BUST MY BUNS TO FINISH CHANGING THESE SKETCHES AND HE DISAPPEARS!

I CAN'T FIGURE THAT GUY OUT, EDEN.

TAKE MY WORD FOR IT, MYKE -- THAT'S ALL I KNOW.

ON THE ONE HAND, HE'S *B.B. FLEMM*...THE BEST-SELLING *CHILDREN'S AUTHOR* SINCE THE *BROTHERS GRIMM.*

AND ON THE OTHER, HE'S *JON SABLE*...BOUNTY HUNTER, BODYGUARD, ADVENTURER-FOR-HIRE.

HE HAS A *SENSITIVE, FUNNY* SIDE, BUT HE *GUARDS* IT WITH A *HARD-NESS*...A *VIOLENCE* I'VE NEVER SEEN IN A MAN BEFORE.

HE HAS HIS REASONS, MYKE.

WELL, I SURE WISH I KNEW WHAT THEY ARE.

I'M JUST HIS *AGENT,* MYKE.

I'M NOT SURE I CAN ANSWER ALL THOSE QUESTIONS.

WHO IS HE? *WHAT* IS HE? *WHY*--?

BUT MAYBE *THIS* CAN.

1.

BWANA!

MUTU KUJU HAPA!

TOA BUNDOUKI M'KUBWA!

ASANTE.

2

(3.)

A STORM

JON Sable FREELANCE™

created, written, and
illustrated by:
MIKE GRELL

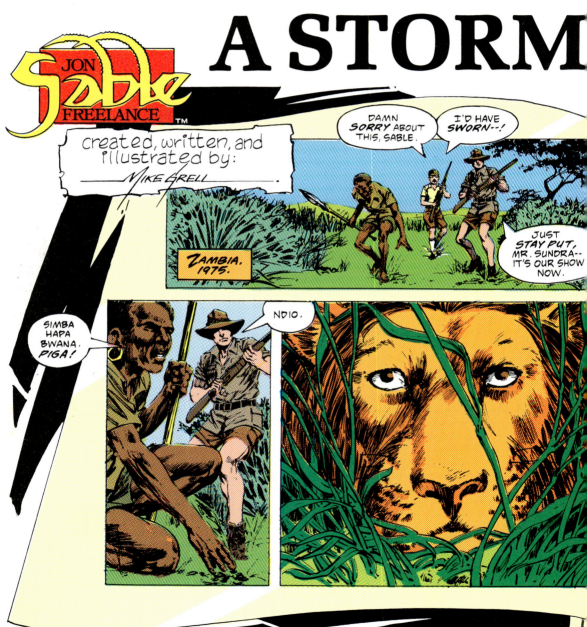

OVER EDEN

AN OLYMPIC RUNNER COVERS ONE HUNDRED METERS IN *TEN SECONDS.*

A *CHARGING LION* DOES IT IN *FOUR.*

AT *TEN FEET,* YOU *POINT* AND *PRAY.*

YOU DON'T FEEL A THING. NO FANGS. NO CLAWS. NOTHING.

JUST A STRANGE KIND OF *BLACKNESS...* LIT BY A FLAME FROM THE PAST.

MUNICH, AUGUST 26, 1972. GÜNTER ZAHN IGNITES THE OLYMPIC FLAME, SIGNALLING THE START OF THE TWENTIETH OLYMPIAD. A WAR-TORN WORLD WATCHES AS THE GREATEST CHAMPIONS OF EVERY NATION GATHER IN THE VERY SHADOW OF DACHAU...

SOME COME FOR *NATIONAL PRIDE...* SOME FOR *PERSONAL GLORY.*

THEY'VE *ALL* COME FOR THE *GOLD.*

COACH TOLD ME ABOUT THIS LITTLE PLACE. IT DATES BACK TO --

YOU SOUND LIKE A *TOURIST,* KID. NOW *THAT--*

--THAT'S WHAT *I* CALL *GREAT* GERMAN ARCHITECTURE!

6

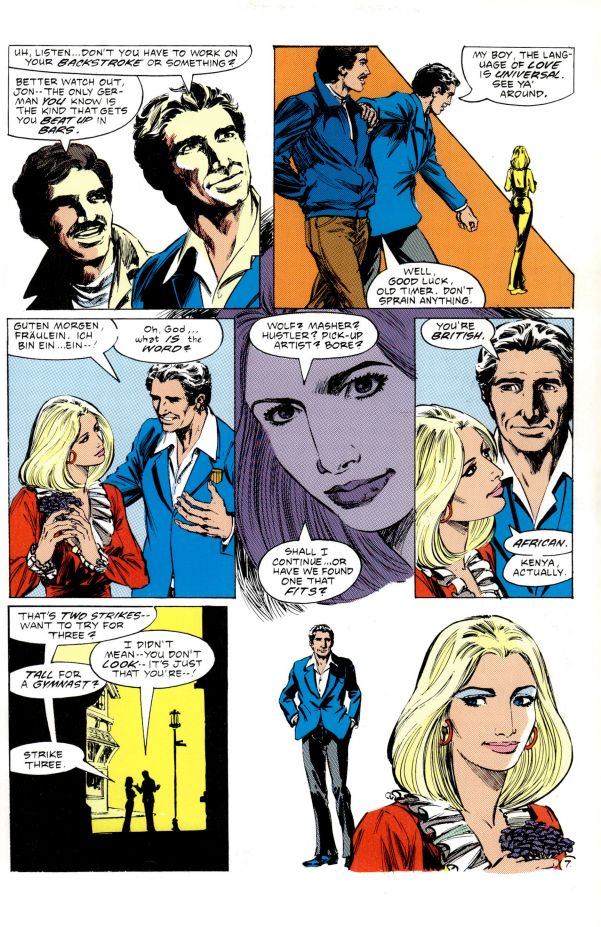

UH, LISTEN...DON'T YOU HAVE TO WORK ON YOUR *BACKSTROKE* OR SOMETHING?

BETTER WATCH OUT, JON--THE ONLY GERMAN *YOU* KNOW IS THE KIND THAT GETS YOU *BEAT UP* IN *BARS.*

MY BOY, THE LANGUAGE OF *LOVE* IS *UNIVERSAL.* SEE YA' AROUND.

WELL, GOOD LUCK, OLD TIMER. DON'T SPRAIN ANYTHING.

GUTEN MORGEN, FRÄULEIN. ICH BIN EIN...EIN--!

Oh, God... what *IS* the *WORD?*

WOLF? MASHER? HUSTLER? PICK-UP ARTIST? BORE?

YOU'RE *BRITISH.*

SHALL I CONTINUE...OR HAVE WE FOUND ONE THAT *FITS?*

AFRICAN. KENYA, ACTUALLY.

THAT'S *TWO STRIKES*-- WANT TO TRY FOR THREE?

I DIDN'T MEAN--YOU DON'T *LOOK*--IT'S JUST THAT YOU'RE--!

TALL FOR A GYMNAST?

STRIKE THREE.

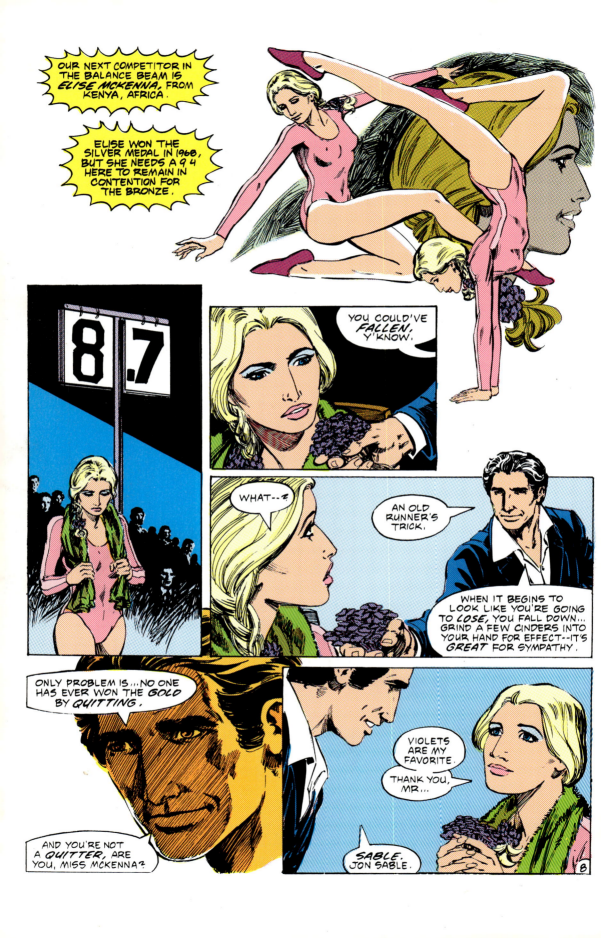

OUR NEXT COMPETITOR IN THE BALANCE BEAM IS *ELISE McKENNA*, FROM KENYA, AFRICA.

ELISE WON THE SILVER MEDAL IN 1968, BUT SHE NEEDS A 9.4 HERE TO REMAIN IN CONTENTION FOR THE BRONZE.

YOU COULD'VE *FALLEN*, Y'KNOW.

WHAT--?

AN OLD RUNNER'S TRICK.

WHEN IT BEGINS TO LOOK LIKE YOU'RE GOING TO *LOSE*, YOU FALL DOWN... GRIND A FEW CINDERS INTO YOUR HAND FOR EFFECT--IT'S *GREAT* FOR SYMPATHY.

ONLY PROBLEM IS ...NO ONE HAS EVER WON THE *GOLD* BY *QUITTING*.

VIOLETS ARE MY FAVORITE.

THANK YOU, MR...

AND YOU'RE NOT A *QUITTER*, ARE YOU, MISS McKENNA?

SABLE. JON SABLE.

B

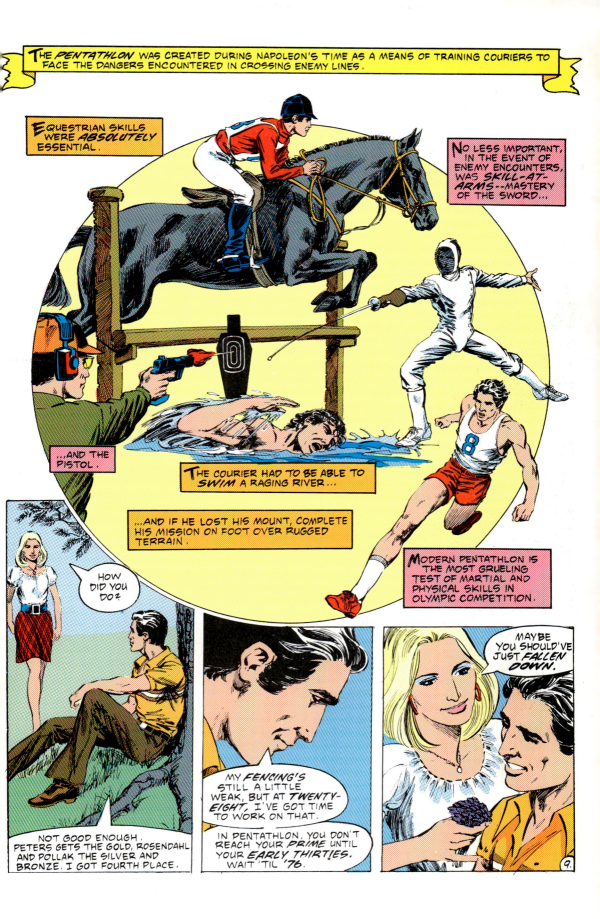

THE *PENTATHLON* WAS CREATED DURING NAPOLEON'S TIME AS A MEANS OF TRAINING COURIERS TO FACE THE DANGERS ENCOUNTERED IN CROSSING ENEMY LINES.

EQUESTRIAN SKILLS WERE *ABSOLUTELY* ESSENTIAL.

NO LESS IMPORTANT, IN THE EVENT OF ENEMY ENCOUNTERS, WAS *SKILL-AT-ARMS*--MASTERY OF THE SWORD...

...AND THE *PISTOL*.

THE COURIER HAD TO BE ABLE TO *SWIM* A RAGING RIVER...

...AND IF HE LOST HIS MOUNT, COMPLETE HIS MISSION ON FOOT OVER RUGGED TERRAIN.

MODERN PENTATHLON IS THE MOST GRUELING TEST OF MARTIAL AND PHYSICAL SKILLS IN OLYMPIC COMPETITION.

HOW DID YOU DO?

MAYBE YOU SHOULD'VE JUST *FALLEN DOWN.*

MY *FENCING'S* STILL A LITTLE WEAK, BUT AT *TWENTY-EIGHT*, I'VE GOT TIME TO WORK ON THAT.

NOT GOOD ENOUGH. PETERS GETS THE GOLD, ROSENDAHL AND POLLAK THE SILVER AND BRONZE. I GOT FOURTH PLACE.

IN PENTATHLON, YOU DON'T REACH YOUR *PRIME* UNTIL YOUR *EARLY THIRTIES.* WAIT 'TIL '76.

9.

I HEARD THEY'RE ACCUSING SOME PENTATHLETES OF TAKING *DRUGS.*

WELL, I GUESS FOURTH PLACE HAS ITS *ADVANTAGES*-- WHOEVER HEARD OF *CHEATING TO LOSE?*

THIS IS *IT* FOR ME, JON-- I'M THROUGH COMPETING.

GYMNASTICS BELONG TO GIRLS LIKE OLGA KORBUT NOW.

I'M TOO OLD, TOO TALL... AND TOO *TIRED.*

AT LEAST YOU'VE GOT YOUR SILVER MEDAL FROM '68.

WASHED UP AT TWENTY-ONE, YOU'RE SURE YOU DON'T MIND DINING WITH A *HAS-BEEN?*

NOT IF YOU DON'T MIND DINING WITH A *NEVER-WAS.*

...FATHER WAS WITH THE DIPLOMATIC CORPS POSTED IN NAIROBI AT THE END OF THE WAR.

WHEN HE WAS RECALLED TO LONDON, HE STAYED LONG ENOUGH TO GATHER UP MOTHER AND RESIGN HIS COMMISSION. AFRICA HAS A WAY OF GETTING INTO YOUR BLOOD.

I CAN'T BELIEVE IT--WE'VE TALKED ALL NIGHT AND I NEVER EVEN ASKED YOU WHAT YOU DO WHEN YOU'RE NOT COMPETING, JON.

TRAIN, MOSTLY. BUT THERE'S NO GOVERNMENT SUBSIDY FOR ATHLETES IN THE U.S., SO I DO A LITTLE FREELANCE WRITING FOR A SPORTING MAGAZINE.

I'VE ALWAYS DREAMED OF *HUNTING* IN AFRICA--MAYBE SOMEDAY.

HAVE YOU EVER SEEN A *SABLE?*

ONLY PICTURES.

THEY'RE *MAGNIFICENT* CREATURES... FIERCE AND POWERFUL, WITH GREAT CURVING HORNS. A QUARTER-TON OF BLACK IRON *MUSCLE* THAT WON'T BACK DOWN EVEN FROM A LION.

SABLE.

IT *SUITS* YOU.

10.

WELL...IT'S A LOT NICER THAN BEING NAMED AFTER A *RUSSIAN WEASEL*.

CONNOLLYSTRASSE

WHAT'S GOING ON OVER THERE?

THAT'S THE *ISRAELI* QUARTERS.

THEY'RE DEMONSTRATING ONE OF THE *AD-VANTAGES* TO HAVING COMPETED AND *LOST* ALREADY.

YOU CAN STAY OUT UNTIL...

...*FOUR-THIRTY*, AND NOT HAVE TO WORRY ABOUT SNEAKING BACK INTO THE COMPOUND AFTER *CURFEW*.

NOBODY CARES ABOUT US LOSERS.

EXCEPT US LOSERS.

NO.

BUDUDUDOW

WANT TO STAY UP AND WATCH THE SUN RISE?

11.

FOR EVERY BEGINNING THERE IS AN ENDING.

SOMETIMES THE ENDING COMES TOO SOON...

PARDON ME...

...IF YOU LET IT.

...IS THIS SEAT TAKEN?

JON! WHAT ARE YOU--?

GEE, YOU MEAN THIS ISN'T THE PLANE FOR THE UNITED STATES?

AH, WELL. I WONDER IF YOUR GOVERNMENT IS INTERESTED IN A HOT PENTATHLON PROSPECT FOR '76.

BENEATH THE TREE OF LIFE, TWO HEARTS ENTWINE...TWO LIVES BECOME ONE...AND EVERY DAY IS A NEW BEGINNING.

13

THE BORDERS OF BOTSWANA, ZAMBIA, AND RHODESIA INTERSECT ON THE FINEST HUNTING TERRITORY IN AFRICA... THE IDEAL PLACE FOR A MAN WHO DREAMS OF BECOMING A PROFESSIONAL HUNTER.

JON! IT'S HERE!

IT'S HERE!

CONGRATULATIONS, DARLING.

YOU ARE NOW A PROFESSIONAL WHITE HUNTER.

MRS. SABLE... IF YOU WILL KINDLY DO THE HONORS.

GLADLY, BWANA.

Sable Safaris Ltd.

WE'RE IN BUSINESS.

THERE'S SOMETHING ELSE I HAVE TO TELL YOU, JON.

I'VE BEEN TO SEE DR. KIRK--!

DOCTOR?! YOU O.K.?

OH, I'M FINE...BUT THE BUNNY WILL NEVER BE THE SAME!

I'M PREGGERS.

14.

Let go, dammit.

MY GOD, SABLE! ARE YOU O.K.?

YEAH, I'M O.K.--WISH I COULD SAY THE SAME FOR MY RIFLE.

UH... SABLE? IF YOU DON'T MIND--!

ONE FOR THE FOLKS BACK HOME!

YEAH, AND I'LL BET YOU'RE GOING TO TELL THEM YOU SHOT HIM IN THE FOOT!

BWANA! TEMBO IKO! PIGA! KUFA!

KWENDA! PESE! PESE!

WHAT IS IT?

POACHERS! A FRESH KILL WITH THE TUSKS HACKED OUT.

NO NATIVE TRIBE WOULD LEAVE THIS MUCH MEAT TO ROT.

16

HOURS LATER...

HERE THEY COME.

I'LL HANDLE THE GUNNERS -- YOU JUST BACK ME UP.

YOU'RE UNDER ARREST! THROW DOWN YOUR WEAPONS!

HE'S MAKING A RUN FOR IT! I'LL GET HIM!

JON, DON'T--! JON!

THERE'S ONE THING YOU HAVE TO REMEMBER WHEN YOU'RE HUNTING A MAN...

...SOMETIMES YOUR QUARRY HUNTS BACK.

18

IF YOU'VE EVER WONDERED WHETHER THE BLAST FROM A .375 HOLLAND & HOLLAND MAGNUM FIRED POINT BLANK WILL CUT A MAN IN HALF...

...IT WILL.

ARE YOU ALL RIGHT?

YEAH, I'M O.K. WE... CAUGHT 'EM.

ELISE...HAL BROOKS HAS ASKED ME TO JOIN HIS STAFF AS A GAME CONTROL OFFICER.

THE SAFARI BUSINESS HAS BEEN DROPPING OFF THANKS TO THE BLOODY TERR'S AND THAT DAMNED WAR-- WHAT DO YOU THINK?

WELL, I KNOW A GCO DOESN'T EARN MUCH...

...STILL, THE SECURITY MIGHT BE NICE.

YOU MAY HAVE NOTICED... I'M EVER-SO-SLIGHTLY PREGNANT AGAIN.

YOU AND I DON'T GIVE A DAMN FOR POLITICS, JON. THIS IS WHAT MATTERS.

GOVERNMENTS COME AND GO...BUT THIS GOES ON, SO WILL WE.

19.

SOMETHING'S TROUBLING YOU, JON.

REMEMBER SONNY PRATT-- MY OLD FENCING COACH?

HE SAID I'D NEVER BE A WORLD-CLASS FENCER, BECAUSE I LACKED THE KILLER INSTINCT.

HE WAS WRONG.

ELISE... I KILLED A MAN TODAY.

THE HARD YEARS ARE THE BEST, THE YEARS OF DREAMING, STRUGGLING, BUILDING. THE GOOD OLD DAYS, WHEN THE SIMPLEST PLEASURES ARE THE SWEETEST.

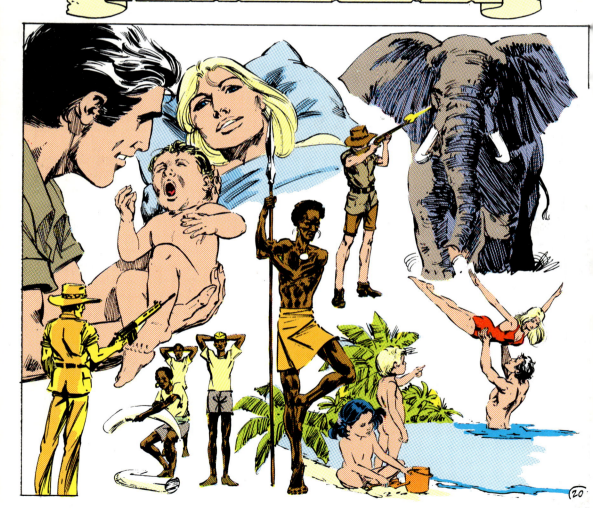

20

JULY, 1978

HAPPY BIRTHDAY!

BERF-DAY!

WHAT DIDJA WISH FOR, MOMMY?

I ALREADY HAVE EVERY-THING I COULD WISH FOR, MARK...

...EXCEPT A BIG KISS FROM YOU AND HEATHER.

UCK! MUSHY!

WHERE DID HE LEARN THAT?

MMM! NOT FROM HIS FATHER, THAT'S FOR SURE.

HERE.

OH, JON! I CAN'T TAKE THIS-- IT'S YOUR LUCKY CHARM!

I DON'T NEED IT ANYMORE.

I'VE GOT YOU AND THE KIDS-- HOW COULD I GET ANY LUCKIER THAN THAT?

21.

ONCE UPON A TIME, IN THE MYTHICAL LAND OF NEW YORK...

WHAT'S "MIFFICAL"?

SHHH!

GET TO THE PART ABOUT THE WINO-- I LIKE THAT BEST.

"DEEP WITHIN THE ENCHANTED FOREST KNOWN AS CENTRAL PARK, THERE WAS A LITTLE HILL CALLED A FAIRY MOUND."

"AND IN THIS FAIRY MOUND THERE LIVED A BAND OF LEPRE-CHAUNS."

"THEY HAD COME FLEEING THE GREAT POTATO FAMINE WHICH THREATENED TO CUT OFF THEIR SUPPLY OF POTEEN, A DESPERATE SITU-ATION, AS ANY IRISHMAN WILL TELL YOU."

"UNFORTU-NATELY, ONCE IN NEW YORK, THEY DIS-COVERED YOU JUST CAN'T GET GOOD HELP ANYMORE. FACED WITH A SEVERE MEMBERSHIP SHORTAGE, THEY WERE FORCED TO BECOME EQUAL OPPOR-TUNITY EMPLOYERS."

"SINCE LEPRECHAUNS BELIEVE EVERYONE IS IRISH IN THEIR HEART, THE ONLY RE-QUIREMENT FOR JOIN-ING WAS THAT YOU MUST BE NO TALLER THAN THE BELLY OF A BEAGLE."

SORRY, BIG FELLOW-- WHY DON'T YOU TRY POUGH-KEEPSIE -- I HEAR THEY'RE HIRING.

22.

"THEIR NEW MEMBERS INCLUDED..."

"...JOSÉ..."

"...KAREEM..."

"...AND BILLY-BOB, WHO CAME FROM SOUTHERN IRELAND... AROUND DALLAS!"

"IN ALL THE LAND, ONLY ONE OF THE BIG FOLK KNEW OF THEIR EXISTENCE."

"J. MICHAEL MURPHY WAS A MAN OF THE WORLD, ACCUSTOMED TO ASSOCIATING WITH BLUE SNAKES AND PINK ELEPHANTS."

"THEY WERE HIS FRIENDS, AND HE WAS THEIR ROLLER COASTER. BESIDES, THEY WERE A DARN SIGHT NICER TO HAVE AROUND THAN THE PURPLE PIG."

YOU'VE LOST THEM, JON.

I HAVE THE ABILITY TO CLOUD CHILDREN'S MINDS.

23

WHERE ARE YOU OFF TO THIS EARLY?

CULLING. HAL RADIOED.

A HERD OF *BUFF* HAVE BEEN RAISING HELL WITH THE CROPS OVER BY THE LUANGWA.

BE CARE-FUL.

ALWAYS.

LOVE YOU.

HERD CULLING HAS NO RELATIONSHIP TO SPORT HUNTING--IT'S A SLAUGHTERHOUSE OPERATION, PLAIN AND SIMPLE. INCREASING HUMAN ENCROACHMENT ON WILDLIFE HABITAT EVENTUALLY LEADS TO TROUBLE...FOR THE ANIMALS.

IT'S NOT FAIR. IT'S JUST THE WAY THINGS ARE.

IT'S BEST IF YOU DON'T *THINK* ABOUT IT.

24

IGNORE THE NOISE!
IGNORE THE RECOIL!

FIRE! RELOAD! FIRE!
AGAIN AND AGAIN!

SAVE THE RIGHT BARREL.

YOU KNOW WHAT'S COMING.

25.

HE'S NOT HERE.

TOO BAD.

STILL, I'LL WAGER THE *IVORY TRADE* IS GOING TO *IMPROVE* IN THIS DISTRICT. 26.

27.

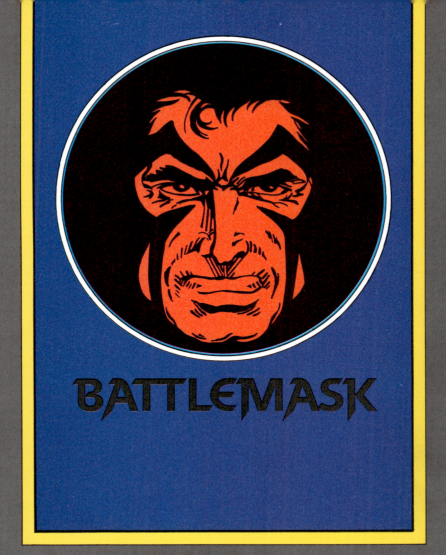

BATTLEMASK

CREATED, WRITTEN
AND ILLUSTRATED BY
MIKE GRELL

EDITED BY
MIKE GOLD

COLORS BY
JANICE COHEN

LETTERS BY
PETER IRO

JULY, 1978.

AFRICAN DAWN STAINS THE SKY AN APPROPRIATE BLOOD RED HUE OVER A PLACE WHERE THE LAUGHTER OF CHILDREN AND THE SOUND OF A SWEET, GENTLE VOICE SHOULD EVEN NOW FILL THE EARLY MORNING HOURS.

INSTEAD, THERE IS DESTRUCTION.

AND DESPAIR.

AND DEATH.

...ELISE...

...MARK...

...HEATHER...

③

COLORIST: JANICE COHEN ✳ LETTERER: PETER IRO ✳ EDITOR: MIKE GOLD

WHEN YOU SET OUT TO HUNT **MAN**, IT'S THE SAME AS WITH **ANY** DANGEROUS PREY.

YOU STUDY THE SPOOR...

...UNTIL YOU GET TO KNOW YOUR QUARRY.

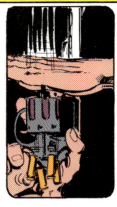

41 MAG R-P

EIGHT MEN! FOUR IN CHEAP JUNGLE BOOTS AND SANDALS...PROBABLY NATIVE.

THREE MORE WITH VIBRAM-SOLED **COMBAT BOOTS**... "EUROPEANS."

THE LAST ONE WORE RIDING BOOTS AND CARRIED A .41 MAGNUM... **NOT** A VERY COMMON CALIBRE

SEVEN AUTOMATIC RIFLES AND ONE PISTOL.

HE'S THE LEADER, ALL RIGHT.

ONE DEAD... SEVEN LEFT-- NOT VERY GOOD ODDS...

...BUT A MAN WITH NOTHING LEFT TO LIVE FOR HAS NOTHING LEFT TO LOSE.

5.

MILE AFTER MILE PASSES SWIFTLY BENEATH THE BURNING AFRICAN SUN--

IMAGES SWIM THROUGH A SWEATY BLUR, AND DEEP INSIDE A SMALL VOICE CRIES OUT, "HURRY, *HURRY!*"

IT'S THE *VOICE* OF VENGEANCE, CRYING OUT FOR BLOOD.

BEFORE THE DAY IS OUT, THERE'LL BE *PLENTY* TO GO AROUND.

7

THERE'S AN EIGHTEEN MILE STRETCH OF THE ZAMBEZI RIVER WITH ONLY ONE CROSSING THAT WON'T LEAVE YOU ARMPIT-DEEP IN CROCODILES.

IT'S JUST TOO BAD HER OLD MAN WASN'T AROUND.

WHO ARE YOU KIDDING, MAN? SHE *KILLED* SAMUEL AND BLEW THE HELL OUT OF *KRAUT*... AND CAME DAMN NEAR TAKING *MY* HEAD OFF--

IF THE GAME OFFICER *HAD* BEEN HOME, WE'D HAVE BEEN *OUTNUMBERED*.

WELL, IT'S A SAFE BET THE GCO WILL UNDERSTAND OUR WARNING.

AND IT'S *STILL* A WASTE... I LIKE A WOMAN WHAT FIGHTS.

8.

9.

10.

THE ZAMBEZI RIVER FLOWS THROUGH SOME OF THE RICHEST GAME LAND IN AFRICA, AND FORMS THE BORDER BETWEEN RHODESIA-- NOW ZIMBABWE-- AND ZAMBIA.

DURING THE LONG, BLOODY WARFARE THAT WRACKED THE NATION FOR OVER A DECADE, RHODESIA'S NATIONAL PARKS BECAME A PRIME ENTRY ROUTE FOR *GUERILLAS* AND *TERRORISTS*.

AND WITH THEM CAME *POACHERS*, SEEKING TO TAKE ADVANTAGE OF THE TENUOUS POLITICAL SITUATION AND THE EVER-INCREASING PRICE OF IVORY ON THE INTERNATIONAL MARKET.

WITH A SINGLE TUSK BRINGING UPWARDS OF *TEN THOUSAND DOLLARS*, IT WAS WORTH THE RISK.

BOOM

BOOM

ALMOST.

12

THEY SAY THE LAND ALONG THE ZAMBEZI WAS HAUNTED DURING THAT TIME.

SOME SAY IT WAS THE SPIRIT OF AN ELEPHANT AVENGING ITS DEATH AT THE HANDS OF A POACHER.

A LOGICAL ASSUMPTION.

13.

IN TRUTH IT WAS NOT THE *RIVER* THAT WAS HAUNTED, BUT THE *MAN* WHO STALKED ITS BANKS.

HAUNTED BY THE MEMORY OF A SMILE, AND A DREAM OF EDEN LONG DEAD.

HAUNTED BY A QUESTION.

SOMETIMES HE CAME OUT OF THE NIGHT TO ASK IT.

THE QUESTION WAS ALWAYS THE SAME.

DO YOU KNOW THE WHITE HAIRED MAN?

THE ANSWER WAS ALWAYS THE SAME.

"NO."

14.

SALISBURY, RHODESIA -- DECEMBER, 1978.

I'M LOOKING FOR JACOB INYATI!

HELLO, JACOB.

HELLO, HAL.

YOU'VE GOT A LOT OF GUTS -- HAVEN'T YOU HEARD, "SEPARATE BUT UNEQUAL?"

WHAT CAN I DO FOR YOU?

FIND JON SABLE.

HE'S GOT TO COME IN, JACOB...BEFORE HE LOSES HIMSELF ALTOGETHER.

LET ME TELL YOU SOMETHING ABOUT JON SABLE...HE'S MY FRIEND -- YOU KNOW WHAT THAT MEANS IN THIS COUNTRY?

HE NEVER GAVE A DAMN FOR POLITICS...RACIAL OR OTHERWISE.

BEFORE THE HARD TIMES, WE USED TO RUN THE SAFARI BUSINESS LIKE A CARNIVAL FOR THE FAT CAT CLIENTS -- I'D PUT ON A LOINCLOTH AND WAVE MY SPEAR AROUND AND TALK SWAHILI -- HELL, JON USED TO MAKE UP HALF THE WORDS -- AND THEN WE'D LAUGH OUR GUTS OUT AFTER THE HUNT!

15.

SOMEBODY'S GOT TO BRING HIM IN, JACOB. BETTER A FRIEND--!

I'M NOT SURE I *WANT* TO.

I WAS OUT THERE-- I SAW WHAT WAS LEFT OF THAT PLACE.

ALL THOSE EMPTY CARTRIDGES LYING AROUND--THERE WERE EIGHT OF THEM WITH AUTOMATIC WEAPONS... AND ELISE WAS ALONE.

SHE FOUGHT... BUT THEY KILLED HER AND THE CHILD- REN...AND JON TOO, IN A WAY-- THEY DE- STROYED HIS HEART.

MAYBE A FRIEND COULD SAVE WHAT'S LEFT.

MAYBE.

DO YOU THINK YOU CAN FIND HIM?

ARE YOU KIDDING? I TAUGHT THAT BOY EVERYTHING HE KNOWS...

...BUT I DIDN'T TEACH HIM EVERYTHING *I* KNOW.

NEXT MORNING...

16.

DO YOU KNOW THE WHITE HAIRED MAN?

JON! IT'S ME!

J-JACOB?!

FOR GOD'S SAKE, GET A HOLD OF YOUR-SELF, JON.

YOU'RE GETTING A LITTLE CARELESS IN YOUR OLD AGE.

DON'T KID YOURSELF. IF YOU DON'T START *BATHING* MORE OFTEN, YOU WON'T BE ABLE TO SNEAK UP ON *ANYTHING*.

HOW DID YOU FIND ME?

YOU'RE THE ONE WHO'S GETTING CARELESS.

YOU'VE BEEN BACK TO THE HOUSE SO MANY TIMES YOU'VE GOT A PATH WORN.

THANKS FOR THE TIP--I'LL HAVE TO CHANGE MY ROUTE.

NO, JON. IT'S TIME TO COME IN. 17.

I WANT HIM *DEAD*, KRAUT.

IT'S NOT GOING TO BE EASY, SIR.

I'M AWARE OF THAT.

IT APPEARS I *UNDERESTIMATED* MR. SABLE.

IN THE PAST SIX MONTHS HE'S CUT OUR OPERATIONS BY A THIRD.

OUR...CLIENTS WILL NOT TOLERATE THE SHORTAGE MUCH LONGER.

WHAT DO YOU SUGGEST?

A LITTLE *HUNT*...

...WITH *IVORY BAIT.*

19.

HE'S OVER HERE! HE'S OVER HERE!

HOW MANY ARE THERE?

WHILE A .375 MAY NOT SHOOT THROUGH SOLID STEEL...

...IT MOST CERTAINLY WILL SHOOT THROUGH EIGHTEEN INCHES OF WOOD.

AND THEN SOME.

22.

24.

YOU'VE CAUSED ME A GREAT DEAL OF *TROUBLE* OVER THE LAST SIX MONTHS...

...AND COST ME A GREAT DEAL OF *MONEY.*

I SHALL TAKE A GREAT DEAL OF *PLEASURE* IN BLOWING YOUR HEAD OFF.

END OF THE LINE, MR. SABLE.

I'M A LITTLE SURPRISED-- YOUR *WIFE* PUT UP MORE OF A *FIGHT.*

25.

SALISBURY, ZIMBABWE, THE PRESENT.

I TRUST YOU GENTLEMEN ARE AWARE OF THE IMPORTANCE OF THIS MISSION.

YESSIR.

THE MAN WHO IS COMING MUST BE STOPPED *AT ALL COSTS.*

IF HE SHOULD SEE ME... RECOGNIZE ME...

...WELL, I NEEDN'T TELL YOU THAT THE PROBLEMS HE CAUSED IN MY IVORY OPERATION ARE NOTHING...

...COMPARED TO THE DANGER HE PRESENTS TO MY *CURRENT* POSITION.

MEANWHILE, FAR OUT IN THE BUSH...

I DON'T SUPPOSE THERE'S ANY WAY I CAN STOP YOU.

NOT A CHANCE.

YOU KNOW THERE'S STILL A *PRICE* ON YOUR HEAD.

AND THERE'S A LOT OF PEOPLE WHO'D LOVE TO COLLECT IT.

LET THEM TRY.

27.

THEY DID A PRETTY GOOD JOB OF IT LAST YEAR.

YOU WERE NEARLY KILLED.

FORTUNATELY, HAL, BEING NEARLY KILLED...

...IS NOT THE SAME AS BEING A LITTLE BIT PREGNANT.

GOOD LUCK, JON.

YOU'RE A *DAMN* FOOL!

I'LL BE SEEING YOU, HAL.

WISH ME LUCK?

THERE IS NO REPLY EXCEPT FOR THE SOUND OF RECEDING FOOTSTEPS -- THE JUNGLE NIGHT HAS SWALLOWED HIM. *JON SABLE HAS COME HOME!*

NEXT ISSUE: **KILLZONE!**

KILLZONE

CREATED, WRITTEN
AND ILLUSTRATED BY
MIKE GRELL

EDITED BY
MIKE GOLD

COLORS BY
JANICE COHEN

LETTERS BY
PETER IRO

THE DARKNESS HOLDS NO FEAR FOR THE HUNTER.

THE NIGHT CRIES OF THE JUNGLE ECHO WITH VOICES OF THE PAST...

THE GHOSTLY MEMORY OF LAUGHTER AND LOVE...

AND PAIN.

AND LONELINESS.

THE REASSURING WEIGHT OF STEEL IS THE ONLY COMFORT HERE NOW.

IT'S A HELL OF A WAY TO COME HOME.

2.

EVERY NOW AND THEN NATURE GETS FED UP AND TRIES TO CLEANSE THE CITY.

FOR AWHILE, THE STREETS SPARKLE WITH NEON RAINBOWS.

BUT THE CLEANLINESS IS ONLY A MASK.

IT WEARS OFF.

UNDERNEATH, IT'S STILL THE SAME.

A STORM OVER EDEN
BY
JON SABLE

3.

6.

HAH! *THAT'S* THE BEST OFFER YOU'VE MADE YET!

AND IF BY ACCIDENT I SHOULD SURVIVE, AT LEAST I CAN GET MY .375 OUT OF HOCK.

AND HAVE ENOUGH LEFT OVER TO DRINK YOURSELF TO DEATH... IF YOU TRY REAL HARD.

LET'S GO.

THIS ISN'T A HOTEL, YOU KNOW --THEY FROWN ON GUESTS CHECKING OUT EARLY.

I PAID YOUR FINE. YOU'RE SPRUNG.

YOU WERE PRETTY SURE OF YOURSELF.

YOU OKAY?

I COULD USE A *DRINK.*

NO BOOZE UNTIL THE JOB IS *DONE,* UNDER-STAND?

YOU GET THE *SHAKES* OUT IN THE BUSH, AND SOMEBODY WINDS UP *DEAD MEAT.*

IF IT'S YOU, I DON'T GIVE A DAMN-- BUT IT MIGHT JUST BE *ME.*

10.

HOW DO I LOOK?

YOU'LL DO.

AT LEAST YOU *SMELL* BETTER.

THE *HAT* FEELS A LITTLE *SILLY.* DOESN'T *RED* STAND OUT A *BIT?*

IT'S *SUPPOSED TO...* IT'S YOUR *BADGE.* YOU'RE A MERCENARY NOW--THAT MAKES YOU SPECIAL.

YEAH. THAT MEANS I GET SPECIAL *"TREATMENT"* IF I'M CAPTURED, RIGHT?

THAT'S PART OF THE *DANGER,* JONNY... PART OF THE *FUN.*

MEET YOUR CREW, JON...

...CAPTAINS BLAKE, DICKINSON, MARSHALL...

AND SERGEANT TATE.

ONLY SIX OF US?

LARGE FORCE WOULD DRAW TOO MUCH ATTENTION BESIDES...

THE JOB PAYS SIXTY-THOUSAND--NO POINT IN GOING FOR SMALLER SHARES.

"SERGEANT" TATE?

A TEMPORARY SITUATION.

COME MAJORITY RULE, I'LL PROBABLY BE A COLONEL.

BESIDES, I STILL GET EQUAL SHARES NO BIG DEAL.

WELL, IF EVERYBODY ELSE IS A CAPTAIN, WHO'S IN CHARGE?

WHOEVER'S STRONGEST, JONNY.

SADDLE UP!

(11.)

THAT WAS SOME DAMN FINE SHOOTING.

THANKS.

I WASN'T TALKING ABOUT YOU, TAKE A LOOK.

GENTLEMEN, WE ARE ON FOOT.

THAT'S NOT ALL, MILO.

HE GOT MARSHALL, TOO.

DAMN.

WE'VE GOT A SLIGHT PROBLEM HERE, BOYS... THAT PLANE IS SURE TO HAVE RADIOED OUR POSITION. IN ABOUT SIX HOURS WE'RE GOING TO BE UP TO OUR EARS IN GUERRILLAS.

ON THE OTHER HAND, IF WE DON'T GET THOSE PEOPLE OUT, WE DON'T GET PAID.

HELL, MILO -- THE JOB *STILL* PAYS SIXTY THOUSAND DOLLARS, DOESN'T IT?

THAT MEANS OUR SHARES ARE UP TO TWELVE GRAND NOW.

THEY *COULD* GO A LOT *HIGHER*.

THAT'S GOOD ENOUGH FOR ME.

LET'S GO.

THAT'S *NOT* EXACTLY WHAT I *MEANT*.

15.

17.

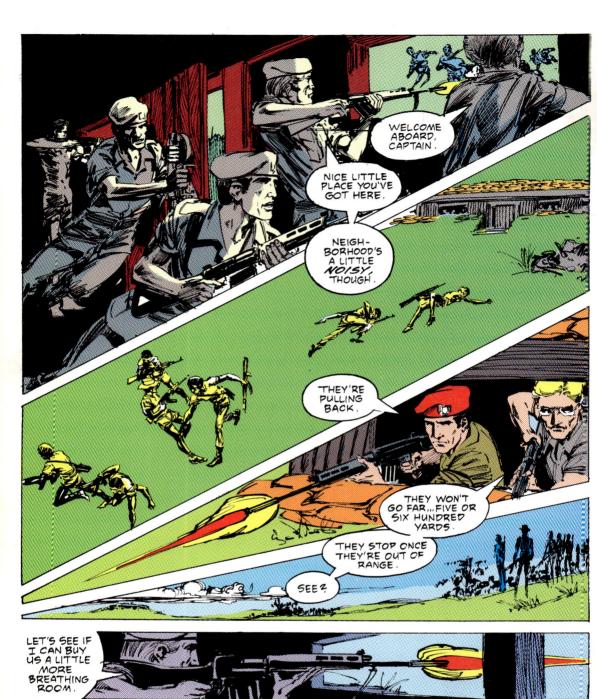

13.

THANKS FOR THE HELP.

OUR PLEASURE -- *SABLE*, ISN'T IT?

MY GOD, MAN -- WE HEARD YOU WERE *DEAD*!

WELL, I DID MY BEST.

AND FROM THE LOOKS OF THINGS OUT THERE, MY OBITUARY WAS ONLY *SLIGHTLY* PREMATURE.

I BELIEVE THESE ARE THE PEOPLE YOU'RE LOOKING FOR.

MR. RAY ARNOLD.

MISS CYNTHIA BISHOP.

AND MR. STEPHEN LAUTER.

WHO'S IN CHARGE HERE?

I AM.

MY FATHER IS SENATOR LAUTER. I DEMAND THAT YOU GET US OUT OF HERE AT ONCE.

WELL NOW, SONNY, IT JUST SO HAPPENS WE'RE HERE FOR THAT VERY PURPOSE.

NOW SHUT UP AND SIT DOWN, AND LET THE GROWN-UPS TALK.

19.

(20.

BALLOON? ARE YOU CRAZY?

WE CAN'T FLY THAT THING IN THIS WIND.

SURE YOU CAN...ITS JUST *DANGEROUS*, THAT'S ALL!

BUT THAT'S KIND OF *RELATIVE* WHEN YOU'RE FACING A HUNDRED ARMED GUERRILLAS.

BUT IT TAKES TOO LONG TO INFLATE.

KID'S GOT A POINT, JON.

THEY'D BE ON US LIKE A DUCK ON A JUNE BUG WHEN THEY SEE THAT THING START TO GO UP.

IT WOULDN'T WORK, ANYWAY.

THE BALLOON CAN ONLY CARRY FOUR.

WELL, I COULD--

I DON'T THINK SO, MILO.

THE SHARES ARE TWENTY THOUSAND APIECE NOW.

I THINK WE'LL STICK TOGETHER.

HAVE IT *YOUR* WAY.

BUT THERE'S NO WAY THAT BALLOON IS GOING TO LIFT SIX PEOPLE.

WE'LL SEE. COME ON.

21.

25.

P--PLEASE...

26.

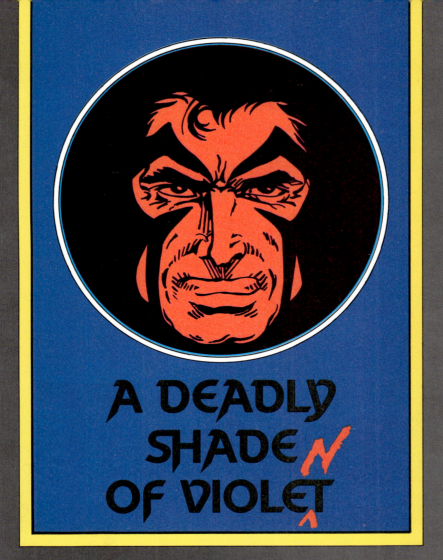

A DEADLY SHADE
OF VIOLET

CREATED, WRITTEN
AND ILLUSTRATED BY
MIKE GRELL

EDITED BY
MIKE GOLD

COLORS BY
BRUCE PATTERSON

LETTERS BY
PETER IRO

FEBRUARY, 1980, WAR TORN RHODESIA STANDS *POISED* ON THE BRINK OF PEACE.

BUT IN THE BUSH, *NOTHING* HAS CHANGED.

LEADING A CIVILIAN ANTI-TERRORIST UNIT IS NO PICNIC.

THE MEN AT YOUR BACK SPEND AS MUCH TIME WATCHING YOU AS LOOKING FOR TERR'S.

...EVER SINCE *MILO JACKSON* LED A PATROL INTO AN AMBUSH.

(1.)

WITH ELECTIONS AT HAND, TERRORISM INCREASED ON ALL SIDES.

SOME OF IT WAS AIMED AT KEEPING VOTERS *AWAY* FROM THE POLLS.

SOME WERE JUST TRYING TO *GRAB* ALL THEY COULD BEFORE THE BUBBLE BURST.

IT ALL BOILED DOWN TO ONE THING.

MORE DIRTY WORK FOR THE *CATU'S.*

2.

THERE'S A SIMPLE RULE FOR SURVIVAL...

...IF THEIR WEAPONS ARE SOVIET-MADE...THE ONES WITH BANANA CLIPS...

..."SHOOT ON SIGHT!

WHEN IN DOUBT, *KILL* 'EM ALL...

...LET GOD SORT 'EM OUT.

SOMETIMES YOU LOSE ONE.

SOMETIMES NOT.

3.

ON APRIL 18, 1980, ZIMBABWE CELEBRATED HER HARD-WON INDEPENDENCE

FORMER OLYMPIC PENTATHLETE.

MISSING FROM THE CROWDS THAT GATHERED IN SALISBURY WAS ONE *SLIGHTLY* USED MERCENARY.

A DEADLY SHADE

NEW YORK, THREE YEARS LATER...

A STORM OVER EDEN
by —JON SABLE.

IT'S NOT ALL HERE, IS IT?

EDEN, THERE'S GOT TO BE SOMETHING *MORE* THAN THIS...

...WHAT HAPPENED TO HIM AFTER AFRICA?

IT'S THAT IMPORTANT TO YOU?

WHAT DO YOU MEAN, MYKE?

DON'T ASK ME WHY.

I DON'T KNOW...I GUESS I JUST CAN'T FIGURE THIS GUY OUT. (8.)

HAVING COMPLETED WHAT YOU'RE SURE IS THE *GREAT AMERICAN NOVEL,* YOU SUBMIT YOUR MASTER-PIECE TO LITERARY AGENTS.

...ONLY *ONE* STAMP...?

AND AFTER AN *INTERMINABLE* WAIT...

POST OFFICE

...YOU BEGIN TO COLLECT *REJECTION SLIPS.*

AND THEN YOU *WAIT* SOME MORE.

THANK YOU

SORRY

TRY AGAIN

NO!

TAKE OFF

REJECTED

GO TO HELL!

DON'T LIKE YOUR LIFE!

NEVER!

F.U.

DON'T CALL US.

FINALLY, FAILING ALL ELSE...

...YOU RESORT TO WORD ASSOCIATION.

TO Ms. EDEN KENDALL

AND...

JON SABLE.

MR. SABLE, THIS IS EDEN KENDALL. I'VE READ YOUR MANUSCRIPT.

CAN YOU COME TO MY OFFICE ON TUESDAY?

10.

UH ... MS. KENDALL--?

BE RIGHT WITH YOU. CAN YOU GIVE ME A HAND?

WANT ME TO TURN THE LADDER?

NO. JUST HAND ME THAT--!

OH! YOU'RE NOT GUS!

WHAT DIDJA THINK?

WELL, FRANKLY, IN TODAY'S MARKET ...

JON, ACTUALLY.

OH, YES, MR. SABLE. I HOPE YOU'LL EXCUSE THE MESS, I'M JUST GETTING SETTLED.

I WANTED TO GET YOU IN AS SOON AS POSSIBLE TO DISCUSS YOUR BOOK.

... "A STORM OVER EDEN" HASN'T GOT A SNOWBALL'S CHANCE IN HELL!

HUH?

11.

OH, IT'S NOT THAT YOUR *WRITING* IS PARTICULARLY BAD.

WELL... WHAT THEN?

HOW'S YOUR TIME STEP?

VERY FUNNY.

THE MARKET IS GLUTTED WITH ACTION-ADVENTURE STORIES RIGHT NOW. I COULDN'T EVEN GET A PUBLISHER TO LOOK AT IT WITHOUT JUMPING UP ON HIS DESK AND DOING A TAPDANCE.

LOOK, MS. KENDALL-- DID YOU CALL ME ALL THE WAY DOWN HERE JUST TO TELL ME THIS?

DIDN'T YOU HAVE TIME TO GET YOUR REJECTION SLIPS PRINTED UP?

I CALLED YOU DOWN HERE, MR. SABLE, BECAUSE I THINK I *CAN* HELP YOU.

REMEMBER THIS SECTION OF THE BOOK?

YOUR KIDS HAD EXCELLENT TASTE. *LEPRECHAUNS* LIVING IN CENTRAL PARK--IT'S A *NATURAL* FOR THE *CHILDREN'S MARKET.*

MR. SABLE... *THIS* I CAN SELL!

YEAH-- THE *BEDTIME STORIES.* MY KIDS ALWAYS GOT A KICK OUT OF THEM.

12.

CHILDREN'S BOOKS?!

YOU'VE GOTTA BE KIDDING!

I'VE ALREADY DRAWN UP A CONTRACT.

NO WAY, LADY.

FACE IT, MR. SABLE...

...I'M YOUR LAST HOPE, OR YOU WOULDN'T BE HERE NOW--PEOPLE DON'T START AT THE *BOTTOM* OF THE LIST!

HOW MUCH IS "A LOT?"

A LOT!

LOOK, THERE'S A LOT OF MONEY IN CHILDREN'S FICTION...

...AND YOU'VE GOT A *SURE THING* THERE.

WILL I HAVE TO USE MY OWN NAME?

USE A PEN NAME IF YOU LIKE.

THERE'S A PLACE FOR IT ON THE CONTRACT. JUST SIGN BOTH SIGNATURES.

DR. SEUSS MADE A FORTUNE ON GRINCHES.

OH, BROTHER.

B. B. FLEMM.

FLEMM?!??

FLEMM?

FLEMM.

13.

THAT WAS THE *CAST* I SAW OF HIM FOR A WHILE.

I WAS BUSY WITH PROMOTION, AND HE JUST NEVER CAME AROUND.

WELL, THAT SOLVES THE MYSTERY OF *B.B. FLEMM*...

BUT HOW DID HE BECOME THIS FREELANCE... *WHATEVER*?

THAT WAS WHEN I HIRED YOU TO ILLUSTRATE THE BOOK.

APPARENTLY, HE DIDN'T SHARE MY ENTHUSIASM.

CONVINCED HE HAD FAILED AS A WRITER, HE TOOK AN APARTMENT IN NEW YORK AND TURNED TO THE ONLY OTHER PROFESSION HE KNEW.

-FREELANCE-
ANYTHING - ANYWHERE
BODYGUARD
BOUNTY-HUNTER
ANYTHING ADVENTUROUS
RHODESIAN EXPERIENCE-
WEAPONS EXPERT
ENQUIRE BOX 1328 THIS PUBLICATION

BLACK ME... FARN TO KI...

HE MUST'VE PULLED A LOT OF *STRINGS* --GOD ONLY KNOWS WHERE HE GOT THE LICENSE FOR A GUN.

ANYTHING IN BOX THIRTEEN TWENTY-EIGHT?

LAST WEEK YOU HAD A *SPIDER*...

BUT HE GOT *LONE-SOME* AND MOVED.

HIS SUCCESS AS A *SOLDIER-OF-FORTUNE* WAS ABOUT EQUAL TO HIS SUCCESS AS A WRITER.

BUT THE SECRET TO STARTING ANY NEW BUSINESS IS *ADVERTISING*.

YOU HAVE TO LET YOUR *CUSTOMERS* KNOW YOU'RE THERE.

NEW YORK POLICE ARE COMBING THE STATE FOR CONVICTED CHILD SLAYER *RICHARD DAHL*.

DAHL *ESCAPED* WHILE BEING TRANSFERRED TO ATTICA STATE PRISON.

14.

TWO WEEKS LATER...

WE'RE OUTSIDE *POLICE HEAD-QUARTERS* WHERE AN ANONYMOUS CALLER HAS SAID THAT ESCAPED CHILD SLAYER RICHARD DAHL WILL BE TURNED OVER TO POLICE CUSTODY--*!*

HERE THEY COME *!*

WHO ARE YOU?

MY NAME IS *JON SABLE*

ARE YOU A POLICE OFFICER?

I WORK STRICTLY *FREELANCE.*

THEN YOU INTEND TO *CLAIM* THE *REWARD* OFFERED FOR DAHL'S CAPTURE?

I'M TOO OLD FOR SANTA CLAUS, AND I DON'T BELIEVE IN BATMAN-- *NO-BODY* DOES THIS KIND OF STUFF FOR FREE.

(15.

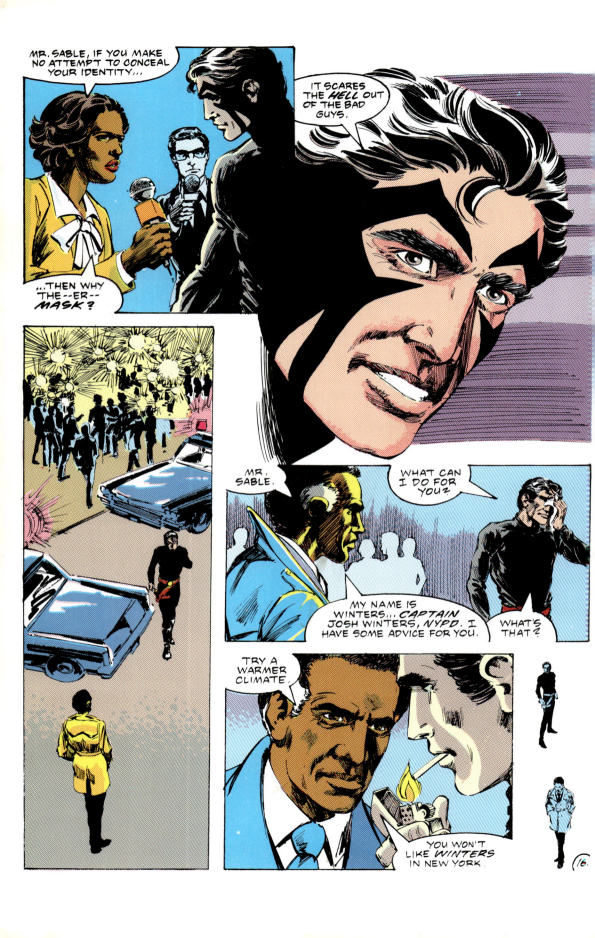

MR. SABLE, IF YOU MAKE NO ATTEMPT TO CONCEAL YOUR IDENTITY...

IT SCARES THE *HELL* OUT OF THE BAD GUYS.

...THEN WHY THE--ER-- *MASK?*

MR. SABLE.

WHAT CAN I DO FOR YOU?

MY NAME IS WINTERS... *CAPTAIN* JOSH WINTERS, *NYPD.* I HAVE SOME ADVICE FOR YOU.

WHAT'S THAT?

TRY A WARMER CLIMATE.

YOU WON'T LIKE *WINTERS* IN NEW YORK.

16.

NEEDLESS TO SAY, *JON SABLE, FREELANCE* SOON HAD ALL THE WORK HE COULD HANDLE.

HE BECAME THE HOTTEST NEWS ITEM SINCE *JACKIE O.*, AND EVERY TIME HE PUT ON THAT MASK THE MEDIA *ATE IT UP.*

IN A MATTER OF WEEKS, CONFIRMED REPORTS HAD HIM IN LONDON, PARIS AND ROME.

RUMORS OF HIS EXPLOITS DEFIED IMAGINATION, AND HE MADE NO EFFORT TO *SQUELCH* THEM... AFTER ALL, IT WAS *GOOD ADVERTISING.*

SABLE.

THIS IS EDEN KENDALL. I'VE BEEN TRYING TO CONTACT YOU FOR WEEKS!

WHERE THE HELL HAVE YOU BEEN?

OUT OF TOWN -- BUSINESS.

YES, I'VE BEEN READING THE PAPERS.

LOOK, NEVER MIND THAT -- I'VE GOT GREAT NEWS...

...I SOLD YOUR BOOK! 17.

BOOK? OH YEAH...WELL... THAT'S NICE.

NICE?!?!

I'LL HAVE YOU KNOW IT'S ONLY A *LITTLE* SHORT OF *FANTASTIC.*

THE PUBLISHER LOVED IT--THEY PUT A *RUSH* ORDER ON THE PRINT JOB TO MAKE THE HOLIDAY RELEASE DATE.

EDEN KENDALL - LITERARY AGENT

AND YOU'VE GOT TO MAKE A PERSONAL APPEARANCE AT *SCRIBNER'S* SATURDAY TO SIGN AUTOGRAPHS.

WAIT A MINUTE. I NEVER *SAID* I'D DO PERSONAL APPEARANCES.

I DID!

READ THE *FINE PRINT* OF YOUR CONTRACT, MR. SABLE,...

...YOU AGREED TO LET ME REPRESENT BOTH YOUR BOOK *AND* YOU.

IF YOU'RE NOT AT THAT STORE, MR. SABLE, I'LL *SUE* YOU FOR EVERYTHING YOU'VE GOT.

AND DON'T BE SUCH A GROUCH--

...I'M GOING TO MAKE YOU A RICH MAN.

AAAARGH!

YOU'RE *WELCOME.* GOOD NIGHT.

18

WHAT DO YOU DO WHEN YOU'VE CAREFULLY BUILT A *REPUTATION* AS A SOLDIER-OF-FORTUNE...

...AND YOUR FACE IS BEING *PLASTERED* ALL OVER THE MEDIA--

...AND YOU SUDDENLY FIND YOURSELF ON THE VERGE OF BECOMING THE BEST-SELLING CHILDREN'S AUTHOR IN THE COUNTRY?

JUST SIGN IT TO, "MY LITTLE FRIEND, BERNICE."

IF YOU'RE JON SABLE--

MEET THE AUTHOR **B.B. FLEMM**

I THINK HE SAID THE "S" WORD.

"...YOU LET *GREED* GET THE BETTER OF YOUR JUDGEMENT.

19.

THE JUNGLE DARKNESS PLAYS STRANGE TRICKS ON YOUR SENSES...

IF YOU STARE LONG ENOUGH...

...THE SHADOWS COME TO LIFE!

21.

ONE OF THE HAZARDS OF AN ALL-NIGHT STAKEOUT IS A CERTAIN *LACK* OF PUBLIC CONVENIENCE.

WHERE THE HELL IS HARRY?

ANSWERING NATURE'S CALL.

HE'S BEEN GONE TOO LONG.

I'M GOING TO HAVE A LOOK.

23.

HE'S HERE--! *'HE'S--!*

HERE.

LISTEN TO ME YOU'RE A DEAD MAN...YOU KNOW THAT.

OH GOD! OH GOD!

GUT SHOT LIKE THAT, YOU COULD LAST A COUPLE OF DAYS--IF THE *HYENAS* DON'T FIND YOU FIRST.

ANSWER A FEW QUESTIONS AND I'LL MAKE IT EASIER FOR YOU.

YOU GUYS HAVE BEEN TRYING TO KILL ME FOR TWO YEARS.

WHY? WHO SENT YOU?

REINHARDT PYKE. HE-- HE'S AFRAID OF YOU.

I NEVER EVEN *HEARD* OF HIM.

OKAY, ONE MORE QUESTION AND YOU GET YOUR REWARD--

--EXACTLY WHERE DO I *FIND* THIS REINHARDT PYKE?

23

SALISBURY, ZIMBABWE.

DRIVING UP TO YOUR ENEMY'S LAIR IN A "SLIGHTLY BORROWED" JEEP IS ONE THING...

...WALKING IN AND RIDING THE ELEVATOR IS ANOTHER.

ARE YOU SURE I CAN'T STAY FOR EVEN A *LITTLE* WHILE?

SORRY, CHERI --I'M EXPECTING...SOME IMPORTANT NEWS. 24.

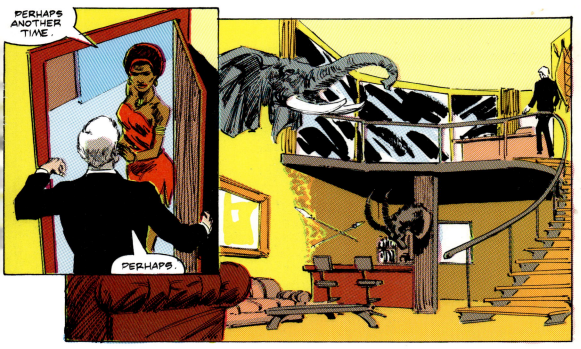

PERHAPS
ANOTHER
TIME.

PERHAPS.

25.

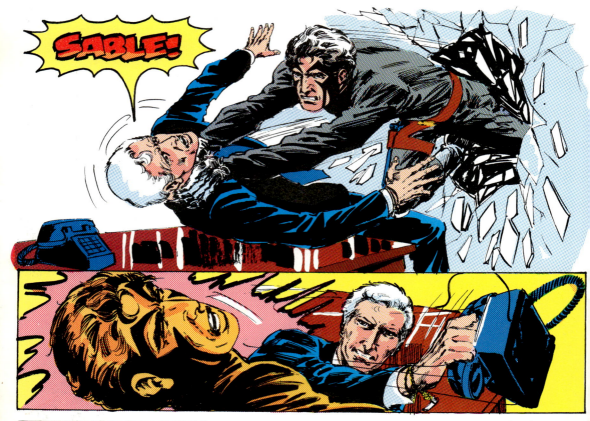

SABLE!

AAAARRR!

THE SEARING PAIN OF A RECENT WOUND NOT YET HEALED BRINGS WAVES OF *NAUSEA* AND *BLINDING AGONY.*

THIS IS FOR THAT LITTLE TRIP DOWN THE RIVER. 26.

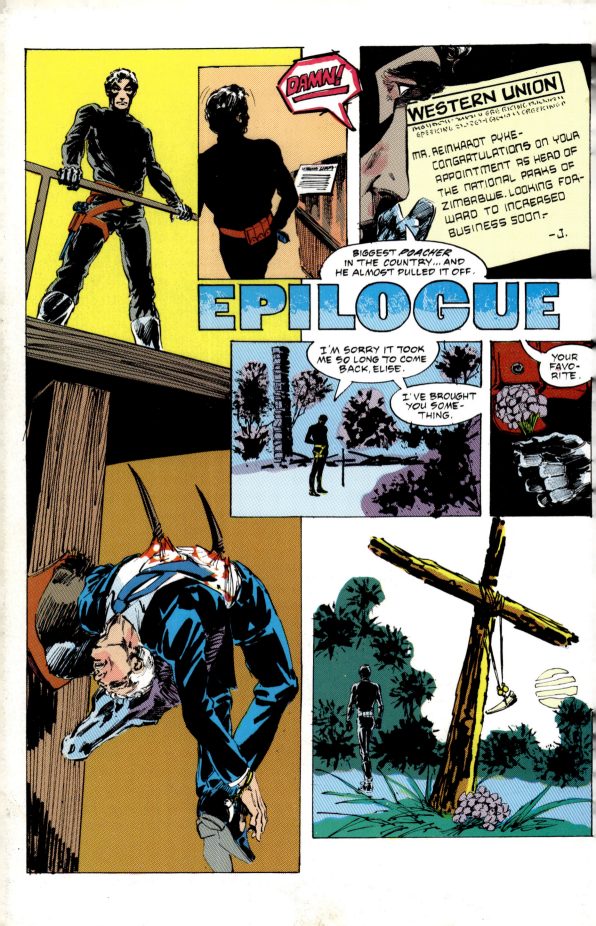

ABOUT THE AUTHOR
by Mike Grell

My real name is Zoltan the Magnificent, and I am the rightful King of the Gypsies. When I was an infant, my family was travelling with a band of our followers through a small town in northern Wisconsin, where I was stolen by a humble woodcutter and his wife, and raised as one of their own.

Being blessed with an active imagination (as you may have guessed) and cursed with an apathetic ineptitude in math, I decided to give up on becoming the next Frank Lloyd Wright and became a cartoonist instead. This was at the suggestion of an Air Force buddy who informed me that "Cartoonists only work two or three days a week, and they make a million dollars a year."

Following a four-year stint as an illustrator with the USAF, I attended the Chicago Academy of Fine Art. While there I began working on comic strip samples, which led to a job working for Dale Messick as an assistant on her classic comic strip, *Brenda Starr*. I drew most everything except Brenda's face, so if I ever write an autobiography it will be entitled *Doing Brenda's Body*.

In 1973 I packed my bags and headed East to take the comic book world by storm, only to find the hatches securely battened. However, I did find a friendly port at D.C. Comics in the form of an editor, Julius Schwartz, who took one look at me and asked the obvious question: "What the hell makes you think you can draw comics?" I walked out a half-hour later with a script in my hand.

My first assignments for D.C. included *Aquaman*, *Superboy and The Legion of Superheroes*, *Batman*, and *Green Lantern and Green Arrow*. In 1974 I created, wrote, and illustrated the first of over fifty issues of *The Warlord*—a title that is still running at D.C. I also created and illustrated *Starslayer* (1981), which was originally published by Pacific Comics, and then by First Comics. From 1981 to 1983 I wrote and drew the *Tarzan* comic strip in the Sunday funnies.

I have just finished a three-issue series for D.C. entitled *The Longbow Hunters*, featuring the Green Arrow character. The first book sold out the day it hit the stands. My next assignments include illustrating Howard Pyle's *Robin Hood* for the Donning Company, and I am currently developing another limited series for D.C., to be published sometime in 1988.

Jon Sable, Freelance speaks for itself, so read. Enjoy.

One more thing—someone owes me $14,000,000.00 and about nine years vacation.